A Shocking
&
Unnatural Incident

GEORGIA ANN MULLEN

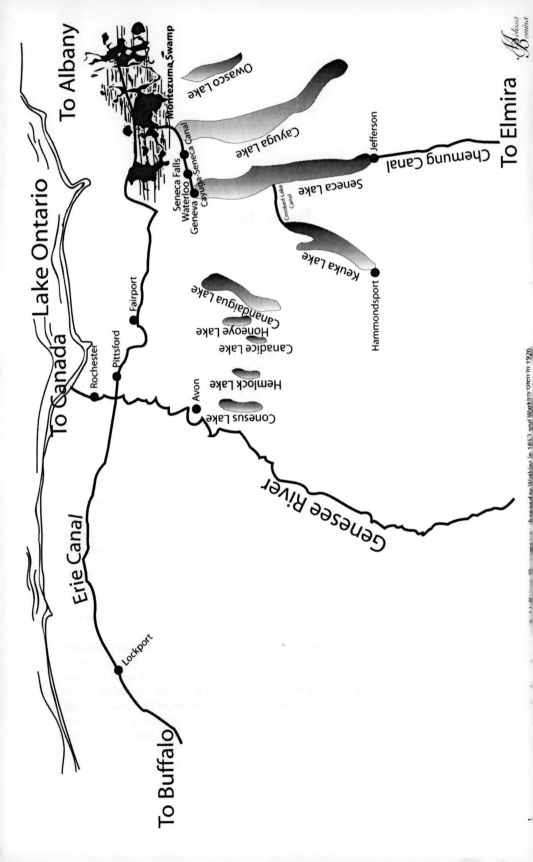

Author's Note

Today we say "women's rights," but 160 years ago the common expression was "woman's rights." In her book *Eighty Years & More*, Elizabeth Cady Stanton labeled her historic 1848 conference in Seneca Falls, New York "The First Woman's Rights Convention." Consequently I refer to it as such. There were also woman's state temperance societies and national woman's rights conventions. Anti-slavery societies were usually referred to as "female," as in the Boston Female Anti-Slavery Society.

PART ONE

CHAPTER ONE

I sprawl on my back like a lazy scarecrow and stare through the barn's rooftop windows. A cloud shaped like a mule's head wiggles long, white ears, and I feel the strong pull of the canal. Across the yard, Ma's in a tizzy, sweeping and dusting, getting our boarding house ready for his royal highness, Abner Manning, the dump's owner. Ma's in an all-fired pucker because I'm not swinging a mop or waving a rag. Beany and her ma are sweating their skin off in the kitchen, cooking up a fancy feast. The smell of chicken frying drifts across the yard and up to my loft. I don't want to sit on command for a big bug like Manning, but if I don't show for dinner Ma's boarders will swallow every piece of chicken right down to the necks.

"Beany! Get your skinny butt in here! BEANY!"

Dread covers me like a blanket. Pa's tipping the corn juice early and starting in on the runt. I roll off my bed, slide down the ladder, run across the yard and get to the kitchen in time to hear Beany whine, "Comin', Mr. Riley."

There she is, the ninny, hopping on one bare foot then the other, squeezing soap from her hands and wiping them on her raggy dress. No wonder he picks on her. Pa leans on the kitchen table close to Beany's ma—too close, as usual. Beany sucks in her lower lip and starts that funny wiggle she does, when she doesn't know whether to yell or run.

"Yeah, Mr. Riley?"

"What you doing?" Pa turns slowly. "Stop prancing and help your ma." He sways and catches the back of a chair. "And keep that mop of hair out of the food. Mr. Manning's coming to dinner. Gonna check us out, and I don't want no mess-ups. We're gonna be picture perfect, ain't we, August?" Pa leans across the table to poke at a bowl of peas, and his bony chest brushes August's shoulder. She doesn't flinch.

"These good?" He paws at the fresh peas with dirty fingers and my stomach rolls, picturing the month's worth of snot under his nails.

"Just picked, Mr. Riley," August says, her potato-peeling knife sliding smooth, like a sled over ice.

Pa straightens up and drags his hand across August's arm. Beany flicks her long, curly hair behind her shoulder, bites her lip and takes a deep breath. I ease into the kitchen and don't take my eyes off my old man.

"Good. Everything's got to be perfect for *Mister* Manning. Big shot new owner. Big shot *Mister* Manning." He grins like there's a joke in there somewhere.

"Everything be fine. Don't you worry." August lifts the corners of her mouth like she sees some humor in him. I don't see nothin' 'cept a weasel huntin' lunch.

Pa throws me a bleary glance, feels his way along the kitchen wall to the back door, stumbles down the porch steps into the weeds and flops down under the big willow tree.

"There he goes, insulting Mother Nature." I watch the willow's long, green leaves swing shut behind him. "Whew! That man's corned again." I slam the door and sit down at the old sawbuck table.

"Yeah, he stink with drink!" August wipes her forehead with the back of her hand.

Beany crosses her skinny arms and cocks her hip—like she's seen me do. "And I hate the way he yells *BEANY! BEANY*! Like I'm deaf or something, and he knows I'm in the washroom scrubbing his dirty drawers!"

I roar like a muleskinner. August giggles and picks up another potato.

"Yeah, but you don't say *boo* to him, do you? '*Comin' Mr. Riley.*'" I ape Beany's whine.

She frowns. "Everybody knows I hate that name Beany. Why does he have to yell it to the world?"

August drops her peeling knife. "That your name, girl. Everybody call you Beany."

"I hate it!"

"Honey, I give you that name!"

"But it don't mean nothin'. What's a *beany?*"

"I tell you that story time after time."

"Don't tell me again, Mama."

"When you born, out you come, all wet, long and skinny like a string bean. 'Cept you ain't green!"

I poke Beany with my finger. "Long, wet and *stringy*. So name her after a *beany!*" The little squirt swats at my hand, but only because her ma's here to protect her.

August pushes the bowl of peas. "Here, honey, run some cold water on these. Give 'em a good rinse."

"And wash his snot off 'em." If I show up for supper, I'll be darn sure to pass on the peas.

Beany fills the bowl with icy pump water, swirls the hard, round little beads with her hand, pours the water off then starts washing the dirt off some spinach.

"Who's this Mr. Manning, Mama? Mr. Hurley owns this house."

"That old coot croaked," I say. "This house went to his daughter, Manning's wife."

"So why's the wife not coming to see it?" Beany asks, shrugging her skinny shoulders.

August stops peeling. "What she got to do with it?"

"She's the owner, right?"

"Honey, she ain't the owner. She's the wife!" Chuckling, August chops the last potato into a heavy black kettle, wipes her knife carefully with a cloth, folds it—strokes the deep blue stone that covers the blade with a sweet touch, like it's precious—and puts it in her torn pocket.

Beany shakes her head. "Mama, your dress is falling apart."

"And yours is over your knees! You growing too fast."

"Hey, Beany, maybe my ma can find you some old lady clothes in the church basement." The kid drops her head and stares at the floor.

"Tessie, don't be mean," August says. "Here, Beany, fill this kettle with water. Put it on the stove. Tess, I hear your mama say he got a daughter."

"Who's got one?"

"Mr. Manning. Maybe she come to dinner."

"What if she does?" I hear rustling in the dining room and keep my eye on the door.

August laughs. "You listen for your mama? You think she gonna come snag you for chores?" She laughs again.

I ignore her. "What about Manning's girl?"

"She a fine young lady."

"What makes her fine, Mama?"

"She rich!"

Beany snorts. She picked that up from me. "Bet she's stuck up. Snooty. All those rich gals got their noses in the air."

"Who says?"

"Tessie." A smile tickles Beany's lips.

"Tessie! Like she know!" August scorns me with a flick of her hand. Beany shakes water from some spinach and stuffs a few leaves into her mouth. The dining room floor creaks and I dash outside, hearing as I flee the door to the kitchen swing with the force of Ma's push. I slide to the porch floor and crouch under a window.

"Have you seen Tess?" Ma bangs two sofa pillows together like she hates them. POK! POK! POK! I know August's covering her precious peas with a cloth. "I asked her to shake these out an hour ago! Where is that girl?"

"She just here…maybe take off for the canal," August says. The tow-path is my favorite hangout—pestering the hoggees to sneak me out of Seneca Falls my main pastime.

"That canal!" Ma pounds the pillows again. "It's given me nothing but heartache. Stole my son. Turned my husband into…" Her words strangle in a dusty cough.

"Maybe she waiting on Cooper," August says calmly. "He coming down from Lockport, right?"

"Yes! And I can't wait to see my darling boy. But there's housework today, and I can't do it alone. *Mister Manning* is coming to dinner!" I peek through the window and see Ma whirl on her heel like a parade soldier, kick the swinging door open and disappear down the hall in a cloud of grumbles and dust. I sneak back into the kitchen.

"You no help to your mama," August scolds, uncovering her vegetables.

"I hate housework."

"Who don't? But it got to be done and you almost grown. What you now, thirteen?"

Three years older than Beany. We grew up together in this boarding house, but we aren't friends. I don't want friends, unless you count the canawlers I hang around with down on the towpath, the whole bunch of us wrestling, flicking knives and cussing. I don't want girl friends—bunch of whiny sissies.

Beany, like most every other kid in Seneca Falls, is afraid of me because I take joy in being wicked. The girls all shrink back, and the boys—they stopped teasing years ago because I smashed 'em all. I can go savage as a meat ax on just about anybody. I like being the town bully but would give it up in a flash to get out of this old town. I offered to take Beany with me—just to have someone to pick on—but she said no. She wasn't leaving her mama and her mama was never leaving Seneca Falls. August always says she's traveled far enough and she's stuck put. Well then, it's Beany's own fault if she's stuck watching my old man paw her mama.

The only person who makes life tolerable for me is Rebecca Harrington, headmistress at the new school for girls, who moved in last summer.

"I've arrived early to become acquainted with the community," she told Ma in her soft voice. "I'll need a room. It doesn't need to be large, just a quiet place to prepare my lessons."

Ma found her a quiet place, all right. She gave Miz Harrington my room and sent me out to the barn. Ma's always looking for a more refined class of boarder.

And Rebecca Harrington is refined! And smart! She's been places and that's what grabbed me. I started right in on her like we were old friends. Where'd she been? What'd she see? Did she bring back something to show me? I was so caught up in that lady's traveling life I hardly said boo when Ma shoved me out to the barn.

"Just for the summer," Ma said. "Someone always leaves by fall, and you'll come back in the house."

Heck no! When I saw how private that barn was and how I could come and go as I pleased, I figured it was a darn good arrangement. Ma tried to get me back inside later like she promised, but I flat-out refused.

Pretty soon I get sick of watching August and Beany fix the grand meal for our honored guest and slip off down to the towpath. I'm dangling my feet in dirty canal water when a sleek, black horse pulls a Dearborn onto the bridge and up the incline toward Fall Street. Turning, I see Ma on our back porch fanning herself with a tea towel. Her usual pale cheeks have a cherry flush. As the carriage passes, a scowling girl with yellow-red hair sticks her head out the window and stares. I pull my feet out of the water, walk around to the front porch and climb onto the railing just as the driver pulls the horse to a halt. Pa is shaking like a rattle on the front step.

The driver hops down, ties the horse to the hitching rail, and opens the carriage door. Carrot Head pops out, crosses her arms, and studies our peeled steps and wilted porch. Okay, our house is not in the best shape. For starters, it's a sad shade of dark green, not any fancier than wet grass, and has a lazy slump in the middle. I've heard town folk joke that the contents of the rooms—beds, bureaus, tables, chairs—slide toward the center. Still, I don't like that snooty gal looking down her nose at it.

Next out is a tall, brawny man in a black suit, followed by a lean boy with pale hair.

"Mr. Manning!" Pa hops off the porch and wobbles like a crippled rooster toward the carriage. "And some of the little Mannings! Welcome!"

Little Mannings! I snort into my shirt sleeve.

"Jeremy, Lucy, this is Mr. Riley. He manages our boarding house." Manning waves them up the flagstone path. Lucy steps carefully over the dandelion leaves creeping over the flat stones like they're slippery banana peels. Manning starts to follow, stops, sticks his nose in the air and sniffs.

"Do I smell alcohol, Mr. Riley?"

"On me? No, sir. Don't touch the stuff. Gave it up years ago. Had a little accident here at the house and swore it off." Manning skewers him with sharp eyes, and Pa's jerky motions stop.

"That's good, Mr. Riley, because I do not allow drinking on the job. And you are employed here, correct?"

"Yes, sir, Mr. Manning. Yes, sir, I'm in charge. Don't worry. You've got a good man here in Liam Riley." Manning holds Pa's eyes a little longer then motions his brats up the porch stairs.

"Whoa!" pale Jeremy teeters as the top step bounces like a raft on a pond.

"I'll fix that in the morning." Pa smiles and his tongue pokes through the hole between his teeth. Lucy gawks like he's a carnival clown. He rubs a hand across his whiskery chin then wipes it on his orange and green checkered vest. Manning looks Pa up and down.

"Clean yourself up, Riley. You're my employee now. I have standards. Don't walk around looking like a bum."

"Yes, sir. No, sir." Pa stares at the ground.

"See to my driver." Manning opens the front door and waves everyone inside. I leave the railing—not one of the big bugs glanced in my direction—and slip up to the front door just as Ma, her dark hair escaping a flyaway bun, hurries into the foyer. She carries the red tea towel and flips it from hand to hand like a sizzling snake.

"How do you do, Mr. Manning? I'm Moira Riley, your housekeeper." She dabs at her forehead.

"I hope you didn't go to too much trouble, Mrs. Riley." Manning glances around the small space.

"Oh, no, no, no. Not a bit." She fans herself lazily.

"These are two of my children. Jeremy and Lucy. My son Freeman is at home with my wife."

Ma looks disappointed. "Oh, your wife couldn't come? That's too bad. But it is nice to meet you, children. The mill girls are washing up. We'll sit down in five minutes. Please make yourselves comfortable. Would you like a cold drink?" Ma's words bounce like popcorn in a skillet. "Some lemonade?"

"No, thank you," Manning replies.

"Children? Lemonade? It's fresh made."

"No, thank..." Jeremy starts to shake his head.

"I'll have some! I love lemonade!" Lucy stares stubbornly at her father. Ooohh, the pouting princess.

Ma motions them into the parlor. "Have a seat, please. I'll be right back with your glass, miss." When she leaves, I open the front door and step inside. Creeping along the foyer wall, I settle onto the stairway's bottom step where I can spy unseen.

Jeremy and Lucy sink onto our old, brown sofa, and Manning folds his stiff black suit into a frayed blue armchair. Ma charges in with a sweating glass of lemonade, offers a quick, "There you go, miss," and whooshes back out.

Our parlor is comfortable, so I don't like the way Manning frowns at the faded wallpaper, chipped woodwork and large, brown water spot on the ceiling. Pa, who's *seen to the driver*, shuffles his feet in the parlor doorway.

"I'll get that fixed, Mr. Manning, first thing tomorrow." Our owner swings his eyes from the ceiling to my old man. "Fixing things costs money, Mr. Manning. Old man Hurley, he..."

The stairway trembles and a gaggle of girls thunders down the steps, their long dresses whipping my face as they push into the dining room and elbow each other for the best seats at the table.

"Hush, girls! Don't sit! Remember, Mr. Manning is here for dinner. Wait by your chairs." Ma, her cheeks rosy with excitement—or maybe just kitchen heat—waves her fancy guests into the dining room.

"Come, please. Dinner's ready."

The Mannings saunter to the table. I leave the step and ease over to the archway separating the dining room and parlor.

"Mr. Manning, you sit at the head of the table, please, as our guest of honor."

Jeremy hangs on a chair near his old man, but Ma says, "Oh, Jeremy, dear, I was hoping Miss Harrington could sit next to your father. Miss Rebecca Harrington is one of our finer boarders," she says in Manning's direction. Ma motions to the teacher, slim in a purple and yellow plaid dress. The old biddies at that other prison of learning—Galworth's School for Girls—never wear anything more exciting than military gray.

"Oh, you have a houseful of fine boarders, Mrs. Riley," Miz Harrington says sweetly. "I'm very pleased to meet you, Mr. Manning." He nods.

Ma takes the chair to Manning's right, and Lucy grabs one next to her, eyeballing Miz Harrington like she's strange and wonderful. Jeremy droops into a chair between two mill girls. One winks at him and wiggles her shoulders. Lucy links eyes briefly with a gal in plain gingham drooling over the princess's fancy dress.

"Liam, time for dinner." Ma waves Pa to the table.

"I washed up." Pa wipes his hands on his pants. His hair sticks to his skull like rotten leaves on a bumpy rock. "Where's Tess?"

"Sshhhh!" Ma frowns. "She'll be along."

Oh, you mean they miss me in all this excitement? I slip into an empty chair at the far end of the table, warning the mill girls with a finger to my lips.

Pa chicken walks to the table and drops into an empty chair. Ma's smile fades. She sniffs the air and her eyebrows bunch but she ignores him and asks Manning to say grace.

Manning offers a swift prayer then everybody starts passing bowls and platters. The mill girls—done sweating out another day at the woolen mill—eat like starved farmhands, shoveling mashed potatoes and swiping soft butter on thick slices of black bread. I snag two chicken legs before the tray empties.

"Please pass the milk," a thin girl mumbles through a mouthful of mushy spinach. Someone hands her a pitcher. "It's empty!"

Ma presses the buzzer under the table and Beany appears at her side. "Two pitchers of milk, please."

Fork floating inches from her mouth, Lucy stares after Beany like she's never seen a colored kid before. In a few seconds, Beany hits the door with her hip and carries in two ironstone pitchers. She sets one near Ma and the other near the wailing milk drinker. I can smell that flowery wash August pours over the kid's hair to make it shine—a sissy girly thing.

"Thank you, Beany." Ma motions her closer and whispers. "Have you seen Tess?" The little snitch raises her eyes in my direction. Ma scowls at me then turns her attention back to the grand Mannings. The mill girls, rubbing their bottomless stomachs, begin to howl.

"Bring more chicken!"

"More bread!"

"More butter, Beany!"

"Butter Bean!"

I glance around to catch who said that.

"Girls! Don't tease," Ma scolds. "I'm sorry, Mr. Manning. Is there anything else you'd like before dessert?"

I slump in my chair, bored and twitchy, while the mill girls polish their plates. Lucy sits poker straight and looks kind of queasy, pulling now and then at the sides of her dress. I've heard some gals her age already wear corsets. Cripes, if she's strapped into one of those contraptions, no wonder she fiddles with her food.

"Every young woman has a right to a good education," I hear Miz Harrington say at the far end of the table. Manning's harsh laugh spins all faces in their direction. He smirks at Miz Harrington, taps his fingertips together and wobbles his head from side to side, making it no secret he thinks the teacher is spouting balderdash. His sneer stretches into a soundless chuckle.

"To a point, my dear," he drawls.

Lucy glares at her old man. "Miss Harrington," she says, "I'm going to college to become a lawyer."

I'm not the only one knocked for a loop. The mill girls giggle.

"You have an excellent goal, Lucy," Miz Harrington says. "Where do you...?"

"Jeremy will be the lawyer." Manning's tone freezes the mill girls' grins. "He'll graduate from Yale, like I did. Lucy, with any luck, will marry a lawyer and raise a nice family in a big house in town. Like her mother did."

Lucy's face flames red as her hair. Her brother slumps wilted as spoiled cabbage between two staring mill girls. Miz Harrington pushes peas around her plate.

The kitchen door swings open and Beany carries four golden pies balanced like squatty pumpkins on her spidery arms. August follows with a tray mounded with spice cookies.

Beany sets one pie down in front of Miz Harrington. "Cherry pie! Thank you, Willow." The mill girls snicker.

Willow! Only Miz Harrington calls her that. And Beany loves it.

CHAPTER TWO

"What you think, Bean?"

"She looked nice."

"Nice!" I snort and flip my pocketknife into the grass. "She looked a little too clean to me. Clean and trussed up like a Sunday chicken." Beany laughs, but August scowls. They eat their cold supper under the willow tree.

"Little shrimpy thing, ain't she? Can't be more than five feet."

"Don't make fun," August scolds. "You don't even know her."

"Yeah, I do. She's rich Lucy Manning. Lives on Washington Street with her rich ma and pa. Oh, I mean her *mother* and *father*. Don't make that face! I know how rich people talk."

The colored cook has a problem kowtowing to white folk. She even kowtows to my old man, a mean drunk. "*Yes, Mister Riley. No, Mister Riley*," she says, looking past his sloppy smile and ignoring the way his hand stumbles over her shoulder or even across her butt! It makes Beany mad, but she never says nothin'. August teaches her real good never to say nothin'.

"You see the way she sat up straight and kept one hand in her lap— like a cripple?" I pick up a chicken leg. "Oh, yeah, and her napkin spread out over that fussy dress. It looked like that fancy pillow Ma brings out at Christmas."

Beany giggles. "I like that pillow."

"And her hair! What color is it anyway? Some mixed-up red?"

"With yellow in it."

"Yeah, mixed-up red-yellow hair! Pulled back in that thick, wavy tail. And that pointy little face. Looked like a fox! Where's my gun?" I laugh and nibble the leg bone.

"She has green eyes."

"How you see her eyes?" August fusses. "You suppose to be serving."

"Green? No kidding."

"Green like marbles—or cat's eyes."

"You both nosy gals."

"She jumped out of that carriage crabby. Stiff as her old man, but that brother's cute." I wink. "You catch him, Beaner?"

"Naw."

"Yeah, you did! Kind of pale but a passable looking boy. Ha! Those mill girls almost had him peeing his pants!"

"Tessie!" August covers her ears. "Shame on you!"

"We should pay him a visit."

"No you don't! Beany, you stay away from those folks."

"Mama, you wanted me to meet that girl."

"No I didn't. Just...just see her. See how a respectable girl act."

I snort, spitting chicken bits at Beany. "Hey! I'm not respectable? I'm not good enough to be friends with your baby Bean, but Miss Priss is?"

"You trouble, Tess. I don't want trouble for Beany. Trouble gonna come her way on its own. She don't have to go looking."

Beany glances at her ma, uneasy. "What's happening on the canal, Tessie?" She inches closer to August.

"Aw, Beaner, You got to come down to the canal!"

"No she don't!" August picks at her straight, white teeth with a long, thick fingernail.

"Cripes, it ain't like she's going to the end of the earth, August! Canal's just out the back door! Beany, there's amazing people on the canal!"

"Half of 'em murderers," August gripes.

"Fancy people? Rich people?"

"No! Real people! There was a guy walked down that plank today—off a packet—was just the kind of guy I'm gonna marry."

"You too young to marry," August butts in.

"Not now! Sweet Jesus! When I'm older."

"And now she taking the Lord's name." August makes the sign of the cross like Ma taught her. August thinks it can ward off evil. I gave up on that religious stuff when I was eight.

"I take it back."

"You should."

"Not the cussing. The marrying. I'm never gonna marry. Every married man I see is a pain in the ass."

"Tessie!"

"What about the guy who walked down the plank?" Beany asks.

"I'm just gonna pal up with him. Well, somebody like him. Someone who's going somewhere."

"Prob'ly to jail." August groans.

"An adventurer! Someone not afraid to hop a boat or a train or a stage coach, not knowing which direction it's heading—north—south—east—west—just jump and go!"

"Sounds like you and him gonna be going in circles." August chuckles. Beany laughs, too.

"Damn!" I knock over the plate of chicken bones. "You got no sense of adventure!" August stops giggling and her face goes mushy. She slumps onto an elbow.

"I done my traveling, girl. All the way from Maryland." Her voice turns watery. "It a long, hard road, and when I get far enough north I say I never gonna travel again, and I don't." When August talks about her long, hard traveling, she always rubs her shoulders. We finish the cherry pie in silence. I stand, ready to leave. August gathers up the plates and forks.

"Ain't your feet hot in those heavy boots?" Like it's her business. "And girl, what you do? Tie your skirt around your ankles? What? You cut that skirt up the middle?"

"Yeah, yeah, forget it."

"You ruin your dress. Turn it into...unmentionables."

"Come on, August, they're pants!"

"Your mama gonna yell! Why you want to dress like a boy, Tessie?"

"It feels good."

"What Miz Riley gonna say when she find out you cut up your clothes?"

"Who cares what she says? I'm going to bed."

"Why you want to dress like a muleskinner?" August grumbles as I head across the yard to the barn. Good, I'm on the right track. Mule driving is just the job I want, just like my brother Cooper.

I climb the ladder to my loft. Feeling my way over to a lamp, I catch a glimpse of night sky through the windows I rigged in the roof and decide not to light it. There'd been a sizable hole in the roof, but now windows keep out the rain and bugs, letting me lie on my bed and star-stare for hours. Coop says people follow the stars when they travel. Can never get lost if you know the stars. 'Course Coop doesn't really need star guides traveling the Erie Canal. He pretty much gets on at one end and floats all the way to the other. 'Course, if the canal springs a leak and all the water pours out taking him with it, he can end up in a cornfield five miles from the slippery waterway.

I kick off my chunky brogans. The heavy, ankle-high work shoes have broad bottoms and big, flat heels and are roomier than any silly girly shoes Ma'd pick for me. The brogans were Coop's before he took off for Buffalo on a canal boat. When he left, my whole life suddenly had hope. Coop sent me letters—short, sketchy and full of strange spelling—but I got his message: There's a big world out there, and I don't have to spend my life docked in Seneca Falls. If I hop a boat east I can get to Montezuma before the captain throws me off. Sneak on again and I'm on the mighty Erie. Before I know it I can be far away from Seneca Falls and people I hate.

Coop did just that. Hopped a freighter four years ago. I watched him go, sniffling back my tears. Last letter, Coop was west of Rochester, riding down the Lockport Five, moving from the high spots to the low.

"It's like tumbling down a waterfall," he wrote, "'cept the boat's safe as a baby's cradle."

And he's not bumming rides now either, catching jobs here and there. Coop has himself a permanent canal job. My brother's a hoggee, driving the long-eared robins that trudge the towpath, pulling the loaded-down cargoes. Coop's earning money—a dollar a day—and right now heading east on the Erie with a load of lumber. His captain is taking a side trip on our little canal and down Seneca Lake to Jefferson with some pickles as a favor to a friend and expects to put up in Seneca Falls any day now. I've been going down to the towpath regularly, watching for him.

The Cayuga-Seneca Canal slips like a skinny snake behind my house and is a drop in the bucket compared to the mighty Erie, but the same rugged toughs pass by going south. I love those guys. A few gals work the canal, too, mostly cooks, but I don't want a cooking job, no thanks. I have my eye on driving mules, nothin' less. That job has power! If it wasn't for the hoggees, who'd move those mules? The mules move the boats. The boats haul the lumber, the salt, the apples, the potash—everything! And it all depends on the hoggees.

I peel off my clothes and shimmy under a thin cotton blanket, raise my arms above my head and look up at the stars, sprinkled like powdered sugar across the sky. My hanging around the canal gets Ma hell-fired. She'd rather I dance behind a broom or take my rage out on a dirty carpet slung across a clothesline. She scorns my spicy canal talk and she hates the Erie for taking Cooper. Hey, hate the man who made Coop leave. I do.

Raindrops skate down the windows, blurring my star search. When he comes home, Coop tells crazy stories about the Erie, his canawler buddies, faraway ports like Pittsford and Medina, and, of course, hell-raising adventures that would make Ma scream if she heard 'em. He saves the hell-raisers for me. Most of his stories are true, but some, I swear, he makes up. Tall tales about swamp ghosts, dancing mules, gigantic water-guzzling squash and fish big enough to pull a boat. Coop knows the darnedest songs, too. Hilarious, raunchy ditties that make Ma cover her ears. I like the one that goes:

"Hoggee on the towpath 5 cents a day,
Picking up mule balls to eat along the way,
Hoggee on the towpath don't know what to say,
Walk behind a mule's behind, all the livelong day."

That's pretty tame compared to some I've heard.

The canal is pure torture for Ma. She says Pa learned all his bad habits as a kid digging the Erie. Mostly, he learned to drink, because booze was on the daily menu. Old timers tell stories about digging the Erie from Albany to Buffalo with little more than picks and shovels and how it made the workers ornery and pigheaded. To urge on an army of worn and weary men, the jigger-boss—just some kid hired for the job—doled out half-gills of whiskey to each laborer sixteen times a day. Coop once talked to an old man who helped dig the Erie's final stretch into Buffalo. The grizzled canawler said the bosses buried kegs of whiskey at regular points along the route the canal would follow. The diggers were egged on with the promise that the next whiskey keg was just around the bend. Dig and you shall drink! Land sakes, I would have given anything to dig the Erie. And I wouldn't have needed booze to spur me on.

I look at my butchered skirt crumpled on the floor. August was right. I did rip that skirt to mid-thigh then work a needle and thread in crude stitches until I formed pant legs. Rawhide strips lash them snug around my ankles. I hate skirts and dresses. Hated them since I first saw how easy boys run, jump and climb without getting wrestled down by yards of cloth. Yep, I like my new look, and nobody is ever gonna get me back in a tangle of petticoats, stockings and buttoned-up shoes for as long as I live.

I stretch, pull the blanket tight around my long body and sigh, content knowing my sweet canal is just outside my door.

CHAPTER THREE

"What you doing, Beanbrain?" The kid's head, a mess of loops, twirls and corkscrew curls, bends low over the kitchen table, and she scratches at something on a piece of old stinky butcher paper. "What you doing, huh?" I poke her hard in the back of the head and her nose bangs the tabletop.

"Ow! Don't, Tessie! I'm writing."

"Writing! You?" I hoot. But, dang, if Beany doesn't put down a stub of pencil and push that bloody paper at me. Pushes it firmly with a *take a look at that!* glint in her chocolate candy eyes. On the paper, letters dance in soft strokes, with swirls at the tops and bottoms. Fancy looking. A lot prettier than my crooked scrawls.

"Miz Harrington's teaching me," she says, rubbing her nose. "She's teaching me to read, too. I have to write this alphabet out five times before she comes home." Beany shoves a stack of papers at me. A few are fancy writing paper with Miz Harrington's initials on top. Others are scraps of paper bags, old envelopes and more butcher paper.

It looks like Beany started out writing the letters school proper, but I can see how, as she got comfortable, she fiddled with them more—fancied them up. Beany doesn't print her alphabet, she draws it. And she's spent a whole page writing out "Willow—Willow—Willow." Nobody calls her Willow, except Miz Harrington. The teacher spent one whole afternoon drawing the little mouse out until she spilled a sob story about hating being called Beany and wishing she had a better name. So Miz Harrington came back with a list of mushy monikers and Beany picked *Willow*. August looked to smack her when the kid said, "*Call me Willow from now on, Mama.*" August refused. And I call her every stupid tree name I can think of—Oak, Sycamore, Cottonwood, Sassafrass—anything to get a rise out of her. Anything but dopey *Willow*.

"What you want with writing?" I nudge Beany's shoulder.

"Stop! You made me mess up."

"Why, huh?"

Beany sticks out her chin. "So I can put down my stories, that's why." She twirls a curl behind her ear.

"What stories?" I nudge her again.

"Ones Mama tells me about her slave days—stop pushing me—and ones I got rolling around in my head."

"You got nothin' rolling around in there but dried beetles you pushed up your nose." She ignores me. "Why you want to write that down any-way—your mama's slave stories?"

She shrugs and leans farther over the paper. "I got to finish. Miz Harrington wants five pages and she'll be home soon. I got one more to go."

"You got more than five pages here already." I flip through the shaggy pile.

"Naw, most of those are just practice. I need five *good* pages to show Miz Harrington."

I drop the pile in disgust. "Hey! I got a letter from Coop today."

"Ummmm."

I was mad as a sweat bee last month when Cooper sailed right past Seneca Falls and didn't stop to see me like he promised. He docked late one night at Montezuma, went with a gang of canawlers into town, and ran right into Pa who, as usual, had a brick in his hat. Pa was up north for one reason only—he found a gin hole that gave him credit. Coop and Pa got into a fra-cas, and the next day Coop never stopped in Seneca Falls. Didn't even get off the boat. Told me about it later in a letter from Hammondsport.

"He's due back here soon."

"Uh, huh." Beany finishes another A to Z, reads the letters over slowly, pointing out each one with her little brown finger, then looks up. "So, how come you're not down by the canal waiting for him?"

"That's where I'm headed. Want to go?"

Beany likes Cooper. When we were little and I did nasty things—tied her up and stuff—Coop usually came and rescued her. I never felt sorry for her. The Bean deserved all she got. She never fought back. Was chicken, poor and simple. Always peeking over her shoulder, expecting trouble. August's the one teaches it to her. That 'fraidy cat stuff. Be careful! Don't go there! Don't do that! You'll get hurt! August always lays a keen eye on Beany, and when they walk to the market—before sunrise—she always makes Beany keep her eyes to the ground, even with no one around but mongrel dogs and daybreak alley cats. I see them. I hear it.

"Never, never look nobody in the eye, hear me, Beany? Mind your own business. Keep your mouth shut." That's what August tells her. Almost like August doesn't want anybody to know she's alive.

I look at Beany's curly brown head bent over the paper. She has way too much hair for one little kid. Tumbling all over her face. If she had some ribbons or something to tie it up, that'd be one thing. But all Beany has is butcher's string.

I hate hair, especially my own. The color's okay. Almost black. Flashier than the usual blah brown. But it's straight as a nail. Stabs my eyes. Ma's always after me to wash it. Who in blazes has time for hair? I've been thinking for a while about whacking it all off.

"Almost done." Beany sets aside another sheet. Miz Harrington is wasting her time. A little colored girl's gonna write down stories? Who'd read 'em anyway?

I straighten out Coop's letter and read over the part about a big fight in Fairport. He'd gotten a black eye and split lip, but said it was nothin' like the bloody, ball-bustin' brawls he fights in Buffalo.

If I'm gonna join him on the Erie, I have to act quick. This morning Ma started in again about school. I didn't go back last September and it about killed her. This morning she said she's saving money to send me to Miz Harrington's academy. Is she kidding? Tess Riley in school with a gaggle of prissy rich gals? Ma said they ain't all rich and certainly not prissy— some are girls just like me. I busted out laughing! If I found even one other girl just like me in Seneca Falls I'd lick a fish!

Ma said she meant some of the girls come from families like mine. Not dirt poor, but not having much. Miz Harrington gives them scholarships, but Ma's saving money all by herself to send me to school.

She puts high value on this new academy because she says it has a "different philosophy and technique." Much as I like Miz Harrington, I doubt her philosophy and technique are different from any other schoolmarm's. They all preach the same: "Sit. Listen. Go home. Come back and do it all over again tomorrow."

Ma says Miz Harrington's school can teach me a lot. She says I need to clean up and not just my clothes. She's always after me to talk right— "*like a higher class of people*"—and not imitate the canawlers' sloppy slang. To me, that higher class is as bland as an empty bird's nest, especially the women. I have no intention of going back to school and getting turned into a stiff-backed whiner. But I am interested in that money Ma's squirreling away.

I leave Beany to her scribbling and hustle down to the canal before Ma can rustle up some dreary housework. Me and women's work? *Not my cup of tea.* How's that for high-class talk?

CHAPTER FOUR

I sit on the back porch watching the packets float by, listening to Beany read "cat" and "dog" to August before they start supper. August is proud of Beany, especially after Miz Harrington said the kid's a fast learner. Beany reads "book," "ship," "log" and "fish" then stops.

"Go on, honey. We got time."

"I can't Mama. I'm scared."

"Why?"

Beany doesn't answer, but I read her mind. It's Saturday and she's worried about the night and Pa coming at August. Beany's chair scrapes the kitchen floor when she stands up.

"I hate him, Mama!"

"Hush, girl! Nothin' for you to worry about."

"I worry about you!"

"Put your book away. We start supper."

"I wish he was dead!"

"Don't say that. Come on now, let's get working."

This is the one thing Beany and I have in common. She was five and me eight when Pa hit Ma in the stomach and killed my little brother. We saw it was a boy baby when it came out too early and too fast. Coop ran for the doctor, but I jumped on Pa, kicking, punching, screaming "Killer! Killer!" He shoved me hard and cracked my head on the wall.

August pushed Pa off Ma—only time I ever saw her touch a white man—and pulled Ma into the little bedroom off the kitchen, calling to Beany to wipe up the blood that poured onto the floor, out from under Ma's dress. It looked sticky and dark. Smelled like something that didn't belong on the outside. Smelled a lot worse than blood on butcher paper.

Liquored-up bad, Pa came after Ma again. He swayed through the bedroom door and August screamed, "Get back, devil!" Then I came running, swinging a fireplace poker and he backed off into the kitchen. August grabbed the poker and threatened Pa herself from the bedroom doorway.

"Get back, demon drunk," she yelled and swung that poker like an ax at Pa's head when he came at her. I guess for a minute she forgot she was colored. Pa ducked and stumbled. Kept calling for Ma, crying he was sorry. Me and August screamed at him and blocked the doorway.

He was tracking back and forth right through Ma's blood, when I couldn't stand the sight of him anymore and ran across the kitchen and punched my head straight into his belly. A big, smelly "*BAAH*" exploded from his gut. It stunk bad, like he'd eaten something dead alongside the road. He turned puke-looking, staggered out the door, and heaved all over the garden. And finally left us alone.

August got a bowl of water and wiped the blood off Ma's legs, and little Beany got back to wiping Ma's mess off the kitchen floor. The rank blood and stink of Pa's puke churned my insides. Prob'ly Beany's, too. I gagged 'til my throat ached. I kept looking out the kitchen door, scared, wondering what Pa would do next. Would he come back inside? Maybe kick me? Or Beany? My heart felt big as a pumpkin and it pounded.

Then Coop came rushing in with the doctor. He looked at Ma lying on the bed, moaning and clutching her belly, then ran back down the street and came back with the constable, who locked up that demon drunk.

The memory's still an ugly sore on my heart. I've hated Pa ever since. So does Cooper. We never forgave Pa for hitting Ma and killing our baby brother. Coop had one mean fight with Pa after another, and, before you knew it, he hopped a canal boat and was off on his big adventure.

I still don't know if Ma ever really forgave Pa for killing her baby boy. She stayed mad at him a long time. He couldn't come to the funeral and see the procession take that tiny casket the long walk through the church. From up front, I saw Beany and August standing in the back watching that coffin no bigger than a cracker box. It was one of the few times I remember them being together in town in broad daylight.

Ma let Pa sit in jail a long time and didn't visit him. Then one day, she got a visit from her priest. The priest told her to forgive Pa. Said he did a very bad thing, but he was her husband and she had to stick with him, no matter what he did. He even made her go to the jail and hear Pa say he was sorry.

It took a few visits from the priest then Pa was back in the house. First, he seemed sorry, hanging around doorways, whispering and making nice. Being the helpful handyman. But soon, he was his old self again, drinking and loafing. Bossing Beany and August. Talking loud and gruff. Little squirt with a big mouth.

But he never hit Ma again, far as I know. After a few months, Ma got back to talking nice to him, but every Saturday night she lights a candle in church and kneels on the cold floor saying her rosary for her dead little babe. August says Ma prays for her worthless husband, too. Says Ma's a patient woman.

And Pa is still a drunk. He usually starts tipping the beer around Friday noon in Waterloo and comes back to Seneca Falls lit up Saturday night. Then he starts looking at August. Ma doesn't know, because she's in church. Soon as she leaves the house, Pa acts up. If August is in the kitchen, he makes some excuse to be there. Getting a piece of pie or a glass of cider—that he spikes real quick with a squirt from a bottle in his pocket. He asks August about the Sunday meal or if the mill girls are eating all the food she puts out. Stupid questions he already knows the answers to because he's always lazing around the house wasting time, except when he's in the saloon boozing.

Yesterday—on a Friday even—Beany and I watched Pa wrap his bony arm around August's waist and stick his mouth on her ear. Beany shocked the shoot out of me when she pushed open the kitchen door so hard it banged the wall. Said, "*Mama, I need you now!*" August pulled away from Pa and followed Beany into their little room, and they locked the door. They were saved on Friday, but there's no doubt in my mind he'll be back tonight.

"Never mind, Mr. Riley, Beany," August says now as they get out the pots and pans. "He just get a little tipsy."

I look through the porch window into the kitchen. Beany stands stiff as a cornstalk. "Why you let him do that?"

"He don't know what he doing."

"Yeah, he does. He's got no business touching you."

Yeah, Pa's pestering August more and more, and Beany's getting more and more sick of it.

CHAPTER FIVE

"Come on! Cripes, you're slow!"

"Stop pulling me!"

"I want to be there when Coop docks up."

"Mama gonna be mad I snuck off with you."

"Stop worrying about what your Mama's gonna be!"

"Why don't you sit on the porch and watch for him?"

"I want to talk to the boys."

"You don't need me for that."

"Well, I can't talk from the porch!"

"You can yell. You got a big mouth...Ow! Don't hit me."

I pull Beany through the yard and down to the towpath.

"Why you so sure Coop's gonna come this time anyway?" Beany rubs her arm. "You been waiting for months, and he's skipped past every other time he promised."

The Bean's getting mouthy. Making speeches even. Usually she has trouble stringing five words together. She's been sassy ever since she learned to read and write. I grab her shabby dress and drag her down the brown dirt path.

"Look! Here comes one now!" A skinny hoggee, a kid not much more than twelve, slows the slap-slap of reins across his mules' dusty backs and brings them to a halt, allowing the packet to glide into shore. The tired folks on board push to the side, eager to get off.

"Hey, Beau! You pot-bellied old fart!" I call to a dumpy guy lazing near the water.

"Tessie!" Beany squeaks. "He gonna slap your head."

"Well, I'll be spavined! Tess Riley! You little guttersnipe." Beau scratches his back on a snubbing post and spits into the water. I open my pocket knife and *THWANG* it into the post.

"Hey, you're getting good." He yanks the knife out and pretends to pitch it into the canal.

"Gimme that, you bum!" I pick up a rock and throw it, just nicking the post near Beau's hip.

"Tessie, hush up."

"You hush up! That's how folks talk down here. If you were worth your weight in potatoes, you'd know it! Hey, Beau, Coop's coming in!" I drag Beany closer to the water.

"Yeah, heard that on the towrope news." He spits again. "Coming in with a load of lumber, is he?"

"Yeah, that's what his last letter said."

"Letter? Coop can write?" Beau smirks.

"'Course he can. Coop's smart...smart enough to get out of Seneca Falls."

"Well, then, you must be a dumb little gal, because you're still hanging around your mama's apron strings." He yanks my hair.

"Am not!" I swipe back. "I'm getting out of here someday soon!"

"Yeah, you are. You're always leaving like greased lightnin', but you're too afraid to leave your mama's kitchen to take up canal life."

"Am not! Coop ain't showed up in months, the skunk. That's why I'm still here." I shove Beau hard and feel Beany pulling at my shirt. "Yeah, yeah! Let's get away from this old bald-headed coot!" Beau laughs.

"He ain't bald, Tessie," Beany says when we get far enough away for her to venture a full sentence.

"He ain't old either, dope. It's just talk."

"Why you talk like that to a man?"

"To a man? What difference does it make if he's a man or a woman or a kid? That's canal life. Rough talk. Hard drink..."

"You don't drink down here!" No, I don't. I hate liquor. But I won't admit anything to Beany.

We spend the next half hour listening to towrope gossip and tall tales from the toughs unloading cargo. Beany falls into a trance hearing those crazy stories. Half of them I'm sure she believes—even the dumb one about the frog with six-foot legs. I imagine her storing those yarns away in the shadowy crannies of her round, dark head. She'll go home and scribble each one on paper and tuck them under her mattress in that miserable little room she shares with August. I offered to let Beany bunk with me in the loft and count the stars, but August won't let her. Says I'll take her baby off on some midnight prowl, which I definitely would.

About six o'clock a hoodledasher comes plowing slowly west, its mule team straining at the harness, the copper-haired hoggee tickling his long-eared robins with the reins, not really hurrying them despite the evening hour.

"Coop!" I shout. The hoggee switches the reins to one hand and shades his eyes. "Cooper!"

I grab Beany's hand and drag her down the dusty towpath. When we reach Coop, I throw my arms around his neck and plant a big kiss on his cheek—then remember my manners and slap him on the back in proper canal fashion.

"Stop it, Tessie, you'll scare my mules." Coop wobbles as I hang on his neck. "I haven't been gone that long." He hugs me, but keeps up a gentle one-hand tap with the reins. The mules plod along like I'm not any more annoying than one more fly.

"It's been months, you bum! You were supposed to come last month and the month before that. Did you lay over someplace or you been sneaking past on the Erie, not coming down the Seneca like you said?"

"Oh, well, a little of both, I guess. I made the Buffalo to Albany run and back a few times. Then I got thrown in jail."

"What for?"

"The usual. Fighting"

"A big, ball-bustin' brawl?"

Coop laughs. "Naw, not that bad. Broke up a rum-hole in Pittsford. Just a bunch of canawlers blowing off steam. Property damage. That's why the sheriff locked us up. If we just busted a couple noses, nobody'd care, unless, of course, some big bug got smashed."

"Where'd you hole up last winter?"

"Albany. Got thrown in jail there, too." He chuckles. "Heard it was gonna be a bad winter, so me and a couple buddies picked a fight—a big one—just so we'd get tossed in the pokey. Was nice to be in a warm jail with three meals a day. Hey, who's that? The Beaner? Hey, gal, you grew up."

The Beaner twists herself like a pretzel and practically buries her head in her armpit, but still comes up with that shy Beany smile.

"Hey, Coop," she whispers, her lips opening and closing over small, white teeth.

Coop looks back at his hoodledasher, one loaded cargo boat with two empties lashed alongside it. "Whoa, Frank. Whoa, Aggie," he drawls, pulling back on the reins.

"Look for a post!" the captain calls. Two husky men scramble across the deck. One loops a rope and swings it over a snubbing post. The hoodledasher coasts in. "Tie 'er up!" the captain orders. Safely secured, the cargo bobs against the side of the canal, while the crew tethers the empty boats, ready for loading, behind it.

"Good job!" the captain shouts. Cooper nods once, winks at me and smiles.

"You done, Coop? Ma's gonna croak when she sees you. You're just in time for supper. Let's hurry. I told Daisy you were coming home."

"Daisy?"

"Yeah, that chubby blond gal. Works in the mill. Crazy for you since first grade. That Daisy."

"Crazy Daisy, huh?" Coop laughs. "Well, I don't need a Crazy Daisy. I got a jularkey in Rochester."

"A what?" Beany squeaks. She's probably wondering how to spell it.

"A sweetheart. Name's Winifred."

"Winifred? What kind of goofy name's that?" I watch the corners of Beany's mouth sink.

"Capt. Beale!" Coop jogs off to talk to the stocky man in baggy pants stepping off the cargo. The captain nods, slaps Coop on the back, and after shouting directions to his crew for unloading the lumber, heads toward town.

"He said I gotta be back at five tomorrow morning."

"Tomorrow!"

"Yeah, can't stay too long."

"Too long? After being gone almost a year, you can't stay more than one day? What's too long for you, Cooper? Two days?" It's always the same. Either he never shows, or he blesses us with his presence overnight and is gone first light.

Coop shrugs and mumbles.

"What?"

"Don't want to make trouble. Don't want to get into it with Pa. You know him and me..."

"To hell with Pa! What about me! And Ma! And Beany!" I throw her in for the heck of it, and her pudding eyes melt with gratitude.

Coop punches my shoulder. "Don't spoil it! I'm here. I'll stay 'til tomorrow, unless you nag me."

I shut pan and we march home. August shouts out the kitchen window and Beany runs inside, apologizing all over the place for leaving August with all the work.

Ma pounces on Cooper, praises the Lord and says she must have had a vision because she's had August make his favorite meal—roasted turkey with all the trimmings. The mill girls gush over Coop like he's the biggest toad in the puddle, cooing over his muscles and saying he needs a haircut. Crazy Daisy reaches up to muss Coop's hair and makes him blush. She's getting girly silly, so I ask, "How's Winifred?" and Daisy says, "Wini-who?" Coop's glare says shut pan.

Supper smells bring the mill girls back to reality, and they abandon Cooper to wolf down another meal. Just as we start passing platters, Pa stumbles into the dining room. He and Coop exchange terse "howdys," nothin' more and everybody relaxes.

After supper Coop treats us to canal stories in the parlor. The one about the dead guy who sat frozen upright in an ice bank all winter long gives everyone the shivers. The one about the drunken pigs sends us rocking in our chairs. I figure Beany, listening on the other side of the parlor door, swallows every word.

"What's Buffalo like?" Daisy asks.

"Mean!" Coop declares with a wicked smile. "A murder a day!"

Ma sucks in her breath. "That can't be true, Cooper."

"Well, every other day."

"I'm going," I stretch my arms wide. "Gimme that canal."

"That canal's not for you! You're just a child...and you're going back to school this fall." School is Ma's daily sermon.

"Yes, Tess. You've promised," Miz Harrington chimes in sweetly.

"Have not! Said I'd think about it."

"You need an education, Tess." Ma's lips set in a thin, tight line.

"I can read and write." I push my flat hair out of my face.

"But there's so much more," Miz Harrington says.

"Yeah, there is, and it's out there." I wave my arm toward the canal. "From Buffalo to Albany and back again. And that's just a little skinny part of it. The world's full of canals and lakes and oceans!"

"Well, you aren't ready for the world, Tessie. You aren't even ready for Buffalo."

I stare at Coop in disbelief. "I'm thirteen. You were ten when you left."

"I was eleven and I'm a guy."

"So?"

"So, the canal's a guy's world. Hard enough for a tough fellow like me. The canal will eat you up overnight. Stay home. Go to school."

"Go to school! I hate school!" I abandon them all and stomp out to the barn. That whole bunch sings like a church choir. Ma. Miz Harrington. Now Cooper. When he comes up to the loft, I ignore him. Just lie on my back, staring out the sky windows. Before he falls asleep on the floor, Coop says he's leaving before dawn. I shouldn't follow him, and he'll drown me if I try.

CHAPTER SIX

It rains all the next day. Big floppy drops splash my windows and beat a dull rhythm on the dark, watery canal. I stay in my loft, doze, read Miz Harrington's travel books, and even though I miss him bad, stay mad at Coop for saying canals aren't for girls. I don't eat all day and am hungry as a hog when I come into the kitchen that evening. I get a welcome wild enough to wake snakes.

"Lordy, Tess!" Ma grabs my shoulders. "Are you hurt?" She runs her hands over my head, checking for gashes and blood. "What happened?"

"I cut my hair, Ma, that's all."

"No! Your hair was beautiful. A little dirty, but..."

"It's still beautiful, Ma. Just short." About ear length all around. I grab some bread and a hunk of meat.

"Have some milk, Tessie." August gives my head the once-over from the sink where she's scrubbing dishes.

"August, look at her," Ma begs, as if August's gaze can bring back my scummy, shaggy, poker-straight, way-too-long hair. It used to hang below my shoulders and was so slippery braids wouldn't hold. I'd forget to cut my bangs for months, and they'd dangle in a heavy black curtain that blocked the sun. Now they're about an inch long and won't be a worry for quite a while.

Beany stares at the wall and dries a glass. I eye her mass of glossy brown curls. When she glances over her shoulder, I grin and snip the air with pretend scissors. Beany snaps her head around and polishes a plate.

"And what is that you're wearing, Tess? Overalls?" Ma's itching for a fight.

"Coop's old ones."

"Sweet Jesus, boys' clothes! That shirt has a hole in the elbow."

"Small one."

"Most of the buttons are missing. Isn't that one of Pa's?"

"Wouldn't wear nothin' of Pa's."

"You look like a boy."

I shrug.

"Where are your skirts and dresses?"

I shrug again. Gnaw a hunk of sandwich. "Don't know. Don't want 'em anyway."

"You'll need them for school this fall."

"Maybe I won't go to school." I pull out my knife, hack off another chunk of meat and start chewing. Ma stares at the blade. First time she's seen it, but she chooses the school fight instead.

"Yes, you will go to school. Everyone says you must. Me. Miss Harrington. Even Cooper, and he knows the value of education, now that he's staring at the backside of a mule sixteen miles a day. Even Coop told you to go to school."

"Yeah, he also told me he whips his weight in wildcats in those mean Buffalo brawls."

"Not Cooper…"

"…and rolls drunks in Albany alleys. He's a bad egg, Ma."

"Tessie, stop plaguing your mama now," August scolds. "Miz Riley, she just cuttin' dideos. We all know Coop's a good boy."

I love Cooper. Mostly because he's no angel. He's a bruiser and a brawler, no doubt about it. The canal stories he shares shock and inspire me. I want Coop's world, bloody, dangerous and work-weary though it is. It beats anything Seneca Falls can offer.

"Coop only told you the good stuff, Ma. You don't think he survives on a nickel a day driving mules, do you?"

"I believe he earns more than a nickel. And he would never attack someone, let alone a drunken person."

"Hey! What you doing here, woman?" Pa stumbles through the doorway, coming up short when he sees Ma at the table.

"Speak of the devil." I frown at my old man, wondering what doggery he fell out of tonight.

Pa's bleary gaze wobbles over to me. "Hey! What happen you? Look like mushroom!"

"Liam! Have you been drinking?"

I snort. "Come on, Ma. Has he been drinking? He can't walk straight and stinks like grog."

Beany glares at Pa. Her dark eyes scrunch into angry slits and dart like summer gnats from Pa to her ma, Pa to her ma.

"You 'spose be church." He sits down at the table—doesn't bother to look for a chair—and claws mightily at the tabletop to keep from landing on his butt. BOOM!

"I never go to church until eight o'clock. How long have you been drinking?"

"Why ain't you church?" Pa repeats, crab-crawling away and banging into the sink.

"For heaven's sake, Liam, get up off the floor!"

"Hello, Mrs. Riley. August. Tess. Willow." Miz Harrington sails into the kitchen with an armload of books and a big smile. "Mr. Riley, may I get you a chair?"

"Naw..." Gobs of spit collect in the corners of his mouth.

"Tess...well, look at you! Isn't that a novel haircut? Won't you be cool when the dog days of summer arrive? Now look here, I found these geography books at the bottom of my trunk. You're interested in exciting new places. Of course, I'll expect book reports when you come to school in September."

"Uh..."

"Just teasing, dear. Enjoy them."

"Tess ain't going school. Get her job at mill, what she need," Pa mumbles, leaning lopsided against the sink.

"We're not discussing Tess' education when you're tipsy, Liam."

"Tipsy! Ma, he's corned! And I am too going to school!"

"Well, I'm glad to hear that, Tess," Miz Harrington says, dumping the stack of books into my arms. "Start right in. Mrs. Riley, is there an old bookcase in the attic she can use?"

"Well..."

"Well, let's go look! Willow, want to come?"

"I ain't going nowhere!"

It's an exclamation—a declaration—and we all stop dead and stare at Beany standing near the kitchen door, chin stuck out defiantly. I haven't seen that much spunk in the Bean in a month of Sundays.

"Go on, honey," August coos. "Go with them. That attic a mystery. Never know what up there."

"I'm staying with you, Mama."

"Go on, honey." She gives Beany that *don't make trouble* look.

"Yeah, Beanbreath, outta here," Pa growls. Beany takes a step forward and crosses her arms. She almost looks tough.

"You come, too, Mama."

"Yes," Miz Harrington says. "Please join us, August."

"Dammit! No church. Now attic." Pa struggles to his feet and lurches away from the sink, arms stretching for the back door. Beany swings it wide open. The booze and missing doorknob send Pa tumbling through the twilight into the garbage cans that clang and bang amid his oaths and curses. Beany smiles tightly and calmly leads us off on our attic assault.

"Some of us are getting together for a temperance meeting Monday night," Miz Harrington says quietly after we've pawed a path through boxes and crates. "Would you like to come along with me, Mrs. Riley?"

"Me? Good heavens no. Why would I go to a temperance meeting?"

"Well...please excuse my boldness..." She smiles shyly. "...but I notice Mr. Riley likes his liquor."

"Oh no, he just had a nip tonight." Ma wipes cobwebs off her chin.

"A nip? Tonight?" I kick the foot of an old oak dresser. "He's corned every night."

"Not every night, Tess."

"Especially Saturday night when you go to church. He starts Friday with a couple nips at O'Brien's, then Brunner's. Then Vicker's back here in town. Then a few more rum-holes, then he crawls into a back alley to finish off a bottle with his booze bum friends. Long before you're lighting your church candle, he's lit up like fireworks on the Fourth of July!"

"Tess!" Ma grabs my arm. "Not in front of everyone."

"You think no one knows?" I yank my arm away. "No one smells him? Or sees his pissy pants?" Ma pulls back, shocked.

"Now, let's not get stormy," Miz Harrington says, squeezing between us. "There are alternatives. That's what the temperance movement is all about."

"And then he starts on August."

"Tessie!" August claps her hands together. A signal she gave me and Beany to shut pan when we were little.

"Starts what with August?" Ma looks around nervously at old chairs and broken lamps.

"Nothin', Miz Riley, nothin' at all. Mr. Riley like his snacks, so he come asking for a piece of pie, that's all."

"Ha! He's after a lot more than a piece of pie. Ain't he Beaner?" Tears puddle in the corners of Beany's eyes.

"Tess! Don't be crude!"

"Ma, why are you so loyal? So blind? You saw how mad he was when he found you in the kitchen. He's a horny old coot."

"All right, we've snooped around this attic long enough," Miz Harrington sings cheerily. She takes Beany and me by our elbows and steers us downstairs.

"You should know, Ma." I call back over my shoulder. "He hasn't changed."

"All right, Tess," Miz Harrington whispers. "Maybe we can help."

Ma and August follow silently down the stairs. Everyone mumbles good night and drifts toward their bedrooms. I escape to my loft and crawl into bed, knowing Ma is already stepping down the sidewalk toward church to light her candle.

CHAPTER SEVEN

Here she is. I wondered if the little fox would come. Lucy Manning and her ma pause just inside our parlor. She's wearing some frilly thing the color of smooshed cranberries. My eyes trace down the line of bright white buttons on her skirt to the toes of her pointy, buttoned shoes—OUCH! I retrace the path, slowly, and when we link eyes, give her my best sneer. She lowers her eyebrows—oh, that scares me—and stalks over to a hard-backed chair near her ma by the fireplace. I grab a handful of cookies and slouch against the wall a couple feet away. Miss Priss might think she owns this boarding house, but I live here and will stand any dang place I please.

Lucy's trussed up like Sunday dinner, and I'm dressed for a picnic. Baggy boys' pants cinched with a hank of rope. A frayed red and black striped shirt. My clunky brogans and a slouchy hat Ma says belongs on a horse. Ha! Lucy's the horse, harnessed in that corset. I wear nothin' between my shirt and skin. Never will. I pull out my knife and clean my fingernails just to give the little fox the shivers. To show she ain't scared, she stalks past me to the cookie plate.

"Ladies, may I have your attention," Miz Harrington calls, clapping her hands. "Mrs. Riley has graciously allowed us to use her parlor since the post office floor is being varnished." I wonder if that's true, or if she's finagled a way to get Ma to a temperance meeting.

Lucy sits down. "Mother, a girl of color lives here. Is she a runaway slave?"

"Sshhhh." Her ma frowns and hands her a napkin. "You should wait to be invited before taking sweets."

"I'm not a child, Mother, and besides, *she* took one." Lucy jerks her head like I stole something.

"You know Beany?" Leaning toward her, I wipe my mouth with the back of my hand.

"I...I know of her." She shivers when I sit down next to her, but I give her credit for meeting my eyes. "She served when I was here for dinner with my father and brother."

"Why'd you ask about her?" I rub chocolate frosting off my front teeth.

"I just wondered..."

"Beany, ain't no slave. She was born right here in New York. On a canal boat, she says."

"Oh." Her mouth falls open when I offer her a cookie. "Uh, no, thank you.... Is that colored woman a slave?"

"Don't know if August's freed or not. She won't say." I pause. "Can't deny she was a slave one time or another, though, huh? No coloreds ever came to America because they wanted to."

"Um...probably not."

"All I really know about August is that her bastard owner beat her." Lucy and her ma gasp. "I've seen the results of that...the whippings." Lucy glances at her ma, who shifts in her chair.

"Oh, sorry about the language, ma'am." I'm really not. I like scraping at the fussy upper crust. I stick out my hand, decorated with broken fingernails. "I'm Tess. My ma runs this place. I guess you own it, right?" Miz Manning takes my hand slowly.

"Well, yes...sort of...my husband..."

"Ladies!" Miz Harrington claps her hands again. "We keep getting sidetracked. Quiet, please...thank you. One purpose of this meeting is to organize a campaign in Seneca Falls and Waterloo to support the larger state temperance petition being circulated. It will be presented to the legislature on October 1. Mrs. Manning has copies. Each of you will canvass two streets by July 1. Two streets are not much, and we must do our part to eliminate this drunken scourge from our lives. And if not from our personal lives, from the lives of women and children who are brutalized by liquor-soaked husbands and fathers. These defenseless victims are dependent upon their husbands..."

"As we are dependent upon ours," a woman in front of us chimes sweetly. Several women nod. Others frown.

"That is true, Mrs. Stanton. That is one reason I will never marry," Miz Harrington says cheerily.

"Me either," I shout. "I ain't never gonna marry no man!" Several women turn around and gawk. Lucy stares at her knees.

"That is certainly your right, Tess," Miz Harrington says. "No woman should be forced to marry."

The woman called Miz Stanton twists in her chair to face Miz Manning. "I wish there was something we could do to change Abner's mind about sending Lucy to college."

"Nothing will change his mind about Oberlin," Miz Manning whispers back.

I nudge Lucy. "What's Oberlin?"

She pulls her elbow close to her side. "A college in Ohio."

"What's a college?"

Lucy stares at me like I'm from Mongolia—a faraway place I read about in one of Miz Harrington's books. "Oberlin is a school of higher learning."

I laugh. "You want higher learning?"

"Yes."

"You like school?"

"Yes."

"So, you'd say you're smart?"

"Yes. Yes, I would," Lucy hisses, not hiding her temper.

"So am I. I'm dang smart enough to know I don't want no part of school." I lean back in my chair and snort.

"Girls, please," Miz Manning frowns.

"I intend to be a lawyer," Lucy declares, like it ain't a crazy idea.

"Yeah, I heard that. Who'd go to a woman lawyer?"

"Other women!"

As a group, the temperance ladies stop talking and turn to stare at us.

"Someday there will be women lawyers, dear," Miz Stanton declares, leaning toward me. "And women doctors, women bankers, women ministers." A few ladies throw Miz Stanton dirty looks.

"Women shouldn't interfere in those professional occupations. They must stay within their own true sphere," a large biddy in the first row grumbles, rocking on her rump like a ship in a squall.

"Old lady Clay," I whisper. "What do you expect from a minister's wife?" I jab Lucy again, and she scoots to the far edge of her seat.

Miz Stanton stands up. She's not very tall.

"Do you read the Bible, Mrs. Clay?"

"Of course I do. Daily."

"Then you know the Bible always casts women in inferior positions."

"Mrs. Stanton!" Miz Clay pops out of her seat pretty fast for a fat lady.

"You know the church has always been first to hold women down."

"It is God's word..."

"No, it is man's word!" Miz Stanton stretches taller.

"That is blasphemy!" Miz Clay pushes past Miz Stanton into the foyer, where Ma roots in the closet for the old crank's coat.

"That foolish talk will get you in trouble, Elizabeth," Miz Clay calls as she sails through the front door.

"I hope so," Miz Stanton giggles.

The temperance ladies hum like a lawn full of flies. Miz Manning fans herself with a handkerchief and mumbles something about petitions. Lucy crumbles the last cookie in her upturned palm.

"That Miz Stanton…I like her," I say, with another jab to Lucy's ribs.

CHAPTER EIGHT

"Helloooo! Anybody home? Mrs. Riley? Miss Harrington?"

I pull open the front door but the blast of summer heat on my face isn't as shocking as the sight of Lucy Manning, arms crossed, frowning on the front porch behind her ma and Miz Stanton.

"You looking for Miz Harrington?"

"Yes, dear. I have the best news! I must share it with her immediately! I ran into Mrs. Manning and Lucy on the sidewalk and pulled them along, so I can tell you all at once." Miz Stanton's face is flushed, her black curls damp and tossed. "I feel like scorched milk, but I'm not sure if it's the sunshine or my new adventure."

"You can sit in the parlor. I'll get Miz Harrington."

"Is your mother home, too—Tess—is that your name, dear?"

"Yeah, that's me." Ma walks in looking surprised. "Here's my ma."

"So good to see you, Mrs. Manning, Lucy. Mrs. Stanton, you look overheated. Tess, bring a pitcher of lemonade."

"Water will be fine, dear. Water's the best thing for you."

Miz Stanton sits down, opens the two top buttons of her cotton dress and dabs a pink handkerchief at her forehead. She's still fanning when I return with the water, followed by Miz Harrington.

"Thank the Lord, I'm not wearing a corset," Miz Stanton declares, taking the water glass. "Ladies—my best advice—lose that whalebone! I'd be lying on the ground in a dead faint if I'd hurried back from the *Courier* in this heat all trussed up in harness."

"I thought you went to Waterloo today to have tea with your friend Lucretia," Miz Manning says.

"Who's Lucretia?" I ask, ignoring Ma's frown.

"Lucretia Mott, a Quaker minister friend of mine. An abolitionist," Miz Stanton says.

"A *lady minister*?"

Lucy rolls her eyes. Oh, yeah, I forgot—the *lady lawyer*.

"Yes, there are a few, but only in the Quaker religion."

"So, your visit was pleasant?" Miz Harrington asks.

"Better than pleasant. Something grand happened!" Miz Stanton takes another sip. "We've planned a conference for next week."

"A conference?"

"Who?"

"Why?"

"Lucretia, me, a group of us...a woman's rights conference right here in Seneca Falls! The first of its kind! I just put the announcement in the *County Courier*."

A woman's rights conference? Miz Harrington raises her eyebrows. Ma stares at the dusty tabletops. Miz Manning looks ready to jump and run. I take a step forward, eager to hear more.

"It was so good to see Lucretia again. And I finally met her sister, Martha Wright. We were at Jane Hunt's house, and Jane invited Mary Ann M'Clintock. I wish I'd brought you ladies. And Lucy and Tess!" Oh, yeah, so sorry I missed a tea party.

Miz Stanton says the afternoon started out normal with Miz Mott talking about her travels and quoting from her antislavery speeches. They were just catching up, nibbling sweets. Miz Stanton told her friends about her move from Boston last year and how much she missed the concerts and balls in "*that wonderful city*." She told them about all the planning, buying and dealing she had to do—and even enjoyed—while fixing up the old house her father gave her. From there it went to her abolitionist husband being gone so many months at a time. How she pined for adult conversation. Her frustration at not being able to get reliable servants and having to do so much of the cooking, cleaning and mending herself. Oh, my heart's bleeding. I look at dusty Ma and picture August sweating over pots in the kitchen.

Miz Stanton says she crabbed there's no one to help her with her boys. She has to cart them to different schools and to the dentist all by herself. But her grumbling didn't get on her friends' nerves. No, she says, they agreed with her! They all felt wives—and for that matter daughters, mothers, nieces, aunts, grandmothers, anyone female—are nothing but slaves! Miz Manning gasps, but Lucy's eyes pin Miz Stanton like knives in a target.

"Don't be shocked, ladies!" Miz Stanton says cockily. "Every one of us—me, Mary Ann, Martha, Jane—not only felt the drudgery of married life, but also the complete waste of our intellects and energies on life's tiny things. And I, for one, want to put my energies into solving life's complexities."

"You mean temperance and abolition," Miz Harrington says with spirit.

"More than that! I want to lead the fight for woman's rights!"

"What rights?" Miz Manning asks, eyes troubled.

Miz Stanton hoots. "Exactly! Women have none. But don't let me spoil it. You'll hear a lot more about the lack of those rights and how we intend to seize them next week at the conference. And you are coming, my dears."

"Oh, I'll be there," Miz Harrington says. "Will you come, Mrs. Riley?"

"Well, I don't know. Really, I think I have all the rights I need."

Holy cripe! The woman in the room with the least thinks she's sitting pretty.

"I'll go!" I say eagerly. "We'll go together, Ma." At least she'll get out of the house.

"Well, I don't know. Let me get some lemonade." Ma disappears into the kitchen. Miz Manning looks ready to follow.

"Lucretia and I saw the need for this conference eight years ago after that disastrous antislavery convention in London—when the male delegates refused to let the female delegates be seated."

"You didn't get chairs?" That was pretty rude.

"Oh no, Tess. I mean they wouldn't let us be *seated*—as duly elected delegates—even though we'd been sent to the convention by our bone fide abolitionist societies. We said then that women were respected less than thieves, and we needed to change that. But we came home and got caught up in, for one thing, men's issues—temperance and abolition—and we sank back into the minutia of daily life. Chasing dust balls, putting knees back into torn pants..."

"Elizabeth, you're spoiled. That's what mothers do." Miz Manning smiles.

"That's just what Mary Ann said—at first."

"It's a woman's lot, Lizzie."

"That's what Jane said—at first. And do you know what I say? I can do a lot better! Don't treat this lightly, ladies! You, Rebecca, have it only slightly better than we married women. Miranda, aren't you feeling boxed into a corner?" Miz Manning twirls her wedding ring.

"Lucretia travels, lectures, teaches. She has the respect of the anti-slavery movement. What do you have? What do I have?"

"Mrs. Stanton?" The fox sneaks out of her den. "You said Mrs. Mott lectures. I've never heard a woman speak in public—except my teachers—and Mother says it's not polite."

"Poo polite! It's ridiculous! A mere custom and we treat it like dogma! Except for the Quakers. As a Quaker Mrs. Mott can speak almost anywhere she likes. The Quaker religion does not drape women in the suffocating cloak of silence like other religions do. '*Keep women silent and keep them under control*,' that's the motto of most religions I know."

"Oh, Lizzie!" Miz Manning fusses with her skirt. "Be careful what you say!" I toss a dark look at Lucy's ma. Miz Stanton and I obviously belong to the same church when it comes to religion.

"Be careful, be careful," Miz Stanton mimics, but not unkindly. "That's the problem! Women are too cautious, too afraid of offending men. And as for the cloak of silence, be honest, Miranda! You heard that silly Mrs. Clay at the temperance meeting. '*Women must remain in their own sphere*,'" she squeaks, wiggling her nose like a frightened mouse. I howl and slap my thigh.

"Her sphere? A tiny little circle she runs around in wiping noses, embroidering handkerchiefs, plucking chickens, poking puddings? Running around and around with never a novel thought of her own, only her husband's or father's or son's ideas and goals to applaud and support?"

I'm liking Miz Stanton more and more. Like me, she doesn't take much guff.

"Lizzie, calm down!" Miz Harrington pats her friend's shoulder. "You have many novel thoughts. You're very vocal at our temperance meetings."

"Rebecca! The truth is in front of you! I can *belong* to a temperance society. I can be counted as one who opposes drunken behavior. But according to men, I'm not smart enough to form my own opinions on the subject. To present them and defend them in public. To *take credit* for them!"

Miz Stanton falls back in her chair. Ma returns with glasses and a sweating pitcher of lemonade and starts pouring. Miz Harrington sips thoughtfully. She seems to agree, but the other two—Ma included—inspect their fingernails and fuss with their collars. Lucy stares at Miz Stanton like she's God's own angel.

Miz Stanton takes a long swallow of lemonade then tells us about the pathetic women—worn out with birthing babies and scrubbing floors— who came to her father's law office looking for help. Their husbands drank whiskey day and night, lost their jobs then in fits of rage beat their wives and kids just because they were handy. When I hear that a cold chill crosses my shoulders and I watch Ma, who's glued her eyes to the floor.

She tells about one sorry woman who inherited money from her father, but her worthless husband gambled and drank it away. All of it! One of the worst cases was an old lady whose husband left all his money to his son, but that bum gave his widowed ma barely enough to live on. I look once, then twice, at the tears in Lucy's eyes. It's a sad story, but cripes, I don't peg Miss Priss for a bawler.

"Well, I've traumatized you all." Miz Stanton smiles mischievously. "All my stories aren't that tragic. Some are simply humiliating. Listen to this. Jane Hunt said she can't even control the funds of her own sewing circle, and she's the treasurer! She tried to open an account at the bank for dues and things, but the bank rejected her. Her husband had to open the account in *his* name!"

"Didn't they think she could count?" Lucy grumbles.

"Women can't be trusted to handle money, dear! To bankers, we're simply large children."

"That's how my father treats me. He has his own plan for my life, but it's nothing I'm interested in. He won't help me go to college." Lucy's voice thickens.

"Ah, fathers and daughters." Miz Stanton leans forward in her chair and says that after her brother died, she wanted to replace him in her father's heart. Boys were schooled and courageous, so she studied Greek and galloped her horse like a demon. She went to a fancy academy, the only girl in a class of boys studying Latin and mathematics. For three years she was at the top of the class—in second place. When she ran home from school to show her old man she'd received one of two prizes for top grades in Greek, all he said was, "Ah, you should have been a boy." She says she still cries bitter tears over those words. I sympathize with her but still chuckle to myself, thinking that for all her book learning this lady ain't dull at all.

Miz Stanton says she went on to a girls' academy in Troy, but the courses were too easy and she learned more hanging around her father's law office. One day she asked him why he couldn't do more to help suffering women, and he grabbed his law books and read word for word how the laws gave husbands all the power.

"Father said, '*When you grow up, you must talk to the legislators, Lizzie. If you can persuade them to make new laws, the old ones will be a dead letter.*'"

"So he did hope things would get better for you." Lucy smiles hopefully.

"Oh, maybe. He was a good father. He just preferred sons. God took his only one. I was a poor substitute."

"Elizabeth!" Miz Manning exclaims. "You are no such thing!"

Lucy leans forward in her chair. "Tell us more about the conference next week. I want to go."

"You must go, Lucy. We're going to tackle all the important issues: a woman's right to education, the right to work and earn money."

"And keep money!"

"Exactly! I like the way you think. The right to keep their children."

A confused look crosses Lucy's face. "What?"

Yeah. What?

"Women have no legal right to their children, dear," Miz Stanton says. Lucy's ma twists her fingers and squirms in her seat. "I'm sorry, Miranda, the girl must know. If a husband divorces his wife, the children stay with him." Lucy's mouth drops open. Her ma stares at Miz Stanton like she wishes she'd shut pan.

Miz Stanton shrugs and clears her throat. "But, I'm sure you don't have to worry about that." She goes on to tell us that a woman can't own property, sign a contract, sue in court or write a will. She says these are all ordinary fact-of-life necessities denied women under the excuse that such matters are too tiresome for a woman's delicate brain.

"Inferior brain is what men really mean," Lucy mumbles.

"We know women are not inferior to men!" Miz Stanton declares. "Don't let go of that basic truth, girls. Lean on it in your darkest moments, and there will be many. The United States Constitution says all men are created equal…"

"Now that's the problem!" Lucy stands up quickly, almost knocking over the lemonade pitcher. "It *says* men and it *means* men and *not women*."

"We will change that to read all men *and* women are created equal!" Miz Stanton raises her glass in salute. "Exercise your brains, girls. Test them. Stimulate them daily. Ten years from now you don't want to be wearing that weary, anxious look so common on the faces of most females." Exhausted by her own energy, Miz Stanton falls silent.

"Where will the conference be held?" Miz Harrington asks quietly.

"At the Wesleyan Chapel."

Across the street! I'm going!

"We're inviting speakers. Mary Ann is certain she can get Frederick Douglass to come down from Rochester."

"The former slave?" Miz Manning sounds surprised.

"Yes. If anyone can be sympathetic to our crusade for woman's rights, it would be a former fugitive slave!"

"Oh, it's a *crusade* now," Miz Harrington teases.

"Absolutely! I for one have taken up the flag. Last night I began drawing up resolutions. Declarations of what changes in law and custom are mandatory. What women deserve! What we're willing to fight for!"

"Lizzie! Lizzie!" Miz Manning pats her throat nervously. Ma collects the empty glasses and backs up slowly into the dining room, content with her servant role.

"We're meeting tomorrow afternoon for our first planning session. Are you coming?"

"Me?" Miz Manning squeaks, fussing with her hair. "Oh, no, I couldn't."

"Yes, Mother, go. I want to go."

"I couldn't...no. It wouldn't be...Abner would not...and certainly not you, Lucy."

"Certainly not Lucy?" Miz Stanton frowns. Several long seconds pass. "Well, I'm not going to beg, Miranda. And I'm not going to cause trouble between you and your husband. But if he's the reason you're not joining us...maybe that tells you something."

Miz Stanton tucks her handkerchief into her sleeve and stands.

"It took eight years and an afternoon of griping over tea to rekindle the fire ignited in London. But Miranda, we're going to do it! The battle is on! It's your choice to fight...or not."

"Join the crusade, Mother!"

"Oh, Lucy." Miz Manning glances helplessly about the parlor. "I'm...I'm happy."

"Oh, poo, you are not!" Miz Stanton scoffs, waving her hand. "I had the same upbringing. The same lost opportunities. We start now, Miranda. It may be too late for you and me, but look who's sitting there. What do you want for Lucy?"

And me? What do you want for me, Ma?

CHAPTER NINE

"Look." I shove the *County Courier* across the dining room table. "Here's Miz Stanton's convention." Ma picks up the paper.

"A convention to discuss the social, civil and religious condition and rights of woman," she reads, "will be held in the Wesleyan Chapel at Seneca Falls on the 19th and 20th of July."

"You going?"

"Of course not! I have no idea what they'd even talk about." Ma turns the page. I guess she didn't take to heart all Miz Stanton spouted the other day right here in our parlor.

And I wasn't sure I believed it all either. The convention sounded good coming out of Miz Stanton's mouth, but later the idea of a bunch of gussied-up, rich gals talking about how rough they had it didn't set well. Still, I know Ma would benefit from a few rights.

"It sounds like a good idea—for regular folks, you know?"

"No, I don't know." Ma licks her finger and turns another page.

"Well, you know what she said—how men control everything. Women can't own nothin'. Ma, you should pay attention to this, because everything you work for Pa can take."

She laughs. "I don't have much...and he wouldn't do that."

"Oh, yeah, he's an angel. Don't trust him, Ma. Look at Miz Manning. I got no cozy spot in my heart for rich folk, but look how her husband stole her property. This palace should be hers." I snicker.

"You keep your nose out of other people's business, Tess. And stick around. I need help cleaning the bedrooms."

"I heard at that temperance meeting that Miss Priss..."

"Who?"

"That Manning girl."

"Her name is Lucy, and she is a very polite young lady."

"Yeah, well, she wants to go to college. Her ma inherited a bunch of money from old man Hurley, but Lucy's pa won't use any of it on Lucy.

Says it all goes to the boys. Hey, I don't care a lick for Prissy Lucy, but that ain't fair!"

Ma walks to the hall closet and pulls out a broom and dust mop.

"Miz Harrington's all passionate about this convention."

"I thought she was passionate about education." Ma roots around for a pail.

"And temperance. That's why she held that meeting here, because of you."

"Me?" Ma juggles the broom, mop and pail.

"Yeah, because of Pa's boozing. He doesn't keep it secret."

"I know your father drinks, but he's not abusive like he used to be."

"He keeps the rum-holes in business, Ma. And after he knows you're gone to light your candle, he comes home and starts bothering August."

"Let's not get into that again." Ma stalks to the closet, comes back with a handful of rags and hands me one.

"Pushing himself on her."

"Stop! How can August..."

"Don't blame August! She's a slave who ran away. She won't push off a white man. Even a stinking one like Pa. She's scared of him."

"Scared? He barely speaks to her."

I choke on a snort and toss back the dust rag. "He told her if she wasn't nice to him he'd turn her in."

"To who?"

"Slave catchers!"

"Lordy! Even he wouldn't be that cruel."

"He's a mean drunk. Look what he did to you."

Ma's eyes cloud. "He treats me better now."

"Barely. And he still takes his ugliness out on other people."

I heard Miz Harrington say slave catchers didn't care if a colored person was slave or free. They'd snatch any black man off the street and haul him back down south.

I wait for Ma to burrow in the closet, then sneak out the back door and head for the canal.

CHAPTER TEN

"Who can we get to lead the convention?" the plain Quaker lady asks.

"We'll lead it ourselves, Lucretia," Miz Stanton answers in her bossy voice.

"A woman chairman? Don't be silly, Lizzie," challenges Miz M'Clintock.

A whole bunch of woman's rights ladies are holed up in Miz Stanton's parlor trying to figure out—now that they've decided to hold this convention—just how they're gonna do it. Ma wouldn't come when Miz Harrington asked her along, but I said I'd go. I want to check out the Stanton place, anyway. See from the inside how rich folks live. I'm surprised. Her house isn't anything fancy, but she's painted the floors yellow and that really brightens up the place.

Miz Stanton puts me to work with Miss Priss sorting flyers in piles of a hundred. We have to pass them out to everybody in town. Lucy looks miffed when I stamp over to her table, but I'm glad for the chance to study the little fox.

"When the Philadelphia Female Anti-Slavery Society held its first meeting a few years ago, we asked a colored man to conduct it," Lucretia Mott says. "Since Negroes, idiots and women are classed together in legal documents, we were very glad to get one of our own class to come and aid in forming that society."

Is she kidding? No one busts out laughing and Miz M'Clintock even calls out, "Good for you, Lucretia."

"It's your convention," Lucy says in that snotty, know-it-all-tone she favors. "Can't you lead it yourselves, like Mrs. Stanton says?" She's managed to haul her ma across the yard to the Stanton house—the Mannings live right next door. Now that she's here, Miz Manning is putting her heart into sorting and stacking the thousands of flyers Miz Stanton had printed. She wants every woman in Seneca County to receive a hand-delivered flyer and even sent bundles up to Rochester.

"How is your declaration coming, Elizabeth?" Miz Harrington asks above the lady chatter. She opens another box of flyers and pushes it toward me and Lucy.

Miz Stanton tells how she and the others sat down at Miz M'Clintock's beautiful mahogany table and wrote the first draft. Said it was hard at first because they needed a model to help organize their thoughts and demands.

"Then Lizzie came up with the idea of shaping our resolutions after the Declaration of Independence," Miz M'Clintock says. "Changing a few key words of course."

"And adding a few." Miz Stanton's wink says she's itching for trouble.

"Read it to us, please." Miz Harrington smiles eagerly.

"Well..." Miz Stanton pulls out a large, folded piece of paper from her dress pocket. It's wrinkled and smudged. "How's this? 'We hold these truths to be self-evident; that all men *and women* are created equal; that they are endowed by their Creator with certain inalienable rights...'"

Miz Mott claps and calls it "the speech of angels." She's wearing her silly Quaker bucket bonnet in the house. You won't catch me wearing a hat inside in the summer. I chopped my hair again last week when the heat wave hit, this time real close to my head. These ladies with their pounds of braided, curled, spindled and piled hair must have cricks in their necks from holding it all up.

Miz Stanton continues reading. "...when a long train of abuses... reduce them under absolute Despotism, it is their duty to throw off such Government, and to provide new guards for their future security..."

"Throw off the government? That sounds revolutionary, Lizzie." Miz Manning laughs nervously.

"Mother! You sound just like Father!" Lucy slaps her flyers on the table, and her ma drops her head guiltily.

"I didn't make this up!" Miz Stanton exclaims. "I took that directly from The Declaration of Independence! Why should that sacred document mean less when applied to women? As far as I can tell, the history of mankind is a history of man's absolute tyranny over woman."

Well, men don't scare me, but I have to go along with that. I think of Pa bossing Ma and man-handling August. I cock my head in Miz Stanton's direction because now she's saying something about voting. Pa always gets extra drunk on Election Day, like it's some sort of holiday. Along with the other 364 days of the year.

"Women voting? Oh, Lizzie, I have grave reservations about that," Jane Hunt says.

Miz Stanton flaps her hand angrily. "It's the first right of every citizen," she insists hotly. "We can't vote and for that reason, *we can't hold elected office.*" She pounds the last five words into the tabletop.

Miz Hunt shrugs. "So who wants to be a congressman?"

"I do!" Miz Stanton snaps. "Men make women obey laws passed in Washington when women have no voice in creating them." She turns and grumbles to me and Lucy that murderers have more rights than women.

"In the eyes of the law, girls, women are dead. *Legally dead*!" She shakes her head sadly, but smiles when I tell her that, even though I never give much thought to Congress and laws, I'm absolutely sure no man is ever gonna lord anything over me.

"Change comes slowly, Tess," she says. "Thanks to our new law here in New York a married woman can finally own property, but if she chooses to work—or has to work—the poor soul is still forced to turn her wages—skimpy as they are—over to her husband or father, uncle or brother! I'm surprised not to some strange man on the street!"

Lucy, who usually watches Miz Stanton like a kid eyes a magician, keeps her eyes on her flyers. Being sneaky myself, I get the keen feeling she's hiding something.

"Lizzie, you're becoming hysterical. You'll put yourself in a dead faint," Martha Wright cautions with a grin.

"Oh, please! Hysterical! Men are always accusing women of being *hysterical*, when they are simply voicing an opinion men don't agree with!" Miz Stanton fans herself with a fistful of flyers.

Lucy's head pops up. "I wish we could change all these stupid laws that say women can't do things. Laws that treat women childishly."

"That's exactly it, Lucy. If a woman marries," Miz Stanton jabs the air with her finger, "she must promise obedience to her husband. That makes him, for all purposes, her master. If she disobeys him, he can lock her up! Punish her like a child!" Miz Stanton picks up a large stack of flyers, straightens their edges and slaps them back on the table.

"I have to agree with you," Miz Mott says. "The same men who wring their hands and beat their breasts over the abomination of slavery treat their wives and daughters like property."

"But that's unfair." Lucy pounds both fists on the tabletop and her long, red braid flops up and down like a pony's tail. "Why do men act like women aren't people? They treat us slightly better than they treat their horses. Always telling us what to do. Like we don't have a pinch of intelligence. Saying it's for our *protection*, because we're so *delicate*." Her face is red and her breathing heavy. "I'm sick of being deprived of opportunity because I'm a girl."

What a ninny. Being a girl never held me back.

"That's the irony of it, Lucy. We creatures whom men claim to hold dearest to their hearts are slaves to their every whim! At least I managed to avoid that dishonor."

"Oh, you're the only woman here who escaped servitude, Lizzie?" Miz M'Clintock asks slyly.

"Of course, I didn't. I'm a servant! A female workhorse. But the minister who sanctified my bond still couldn't make me promise obedience!"

"You didn't promise to *'love, honor and obey'*?" Miz Hunt asks in awe.

"I did not."

"Henry didn't insist?"

"If Henry has one good quality—and he has a few—his most admirable is his belief in the equality of women."

That seems to settle everybody down. The ladies go about their counting, folding and sorting, casting admiring—even envious—glances at Elizabeth Cady Stanton. That's what everybody calls her. All three names. I heard her tell Miz Harrington that if someone calls her Mrs. Henry Stanton, she doesn't answer.

"Besides, he knew I'd never marry him if he insisted on *obey*," Miz Stanton whispers to Lucy's ma. "It was a bit difficult convincing the minister, but we prevailed."

"Men do such awful things to women." Lucy's voice has lost its snotty edge in favor of an annoying whine.

"Divorce is the worst," Miz Stanton says. According to her, men set down the rules all in their favor. And if a wife manages to separate from a cruel husband—meaning either she or he moves out of the house—the husband can appoint anyone guardian of his children.

"*His* children!" Lucy sputters. "They belong to both parents. Why can't they live with their mother?"

They might be allowed to live with their mother, Miz Stanton says, but she would have no say in their upbringing. If the father moved out, he could put any male friend or relative—from the banker to the butcher to his shiftless brother—in charge of his children's lives. They'd be forced to obey the codger, even if their mother disagreed with his decisions.

Lucy looks like she's been stomped by a mule. She flops into a chair, so bleak she makes *me* shiver.

"This is nothing for you to worry about, Lucy," Miz Manning says quietly, but the girl looks doubtful.

Miz Harrington walks over to our table. "You've frightened her, Elizabeth."

"Men's sins against married women are frightening," Miz Stanton says grimly.

"Single women don't have it much better," Miz Harrington replies.

"You can manage your own property," Miz Manning moans.

"And I get taxed on it, but have no representation in government," Miz Harrington replies quickly.

"*Taxation without representation*!" Miz Stanton mocks. "Remember how men fought over that?"

"But women are at least represented by elected officials," Miz Manning offers. "Even if they can't hold office themselves."

"Represented?" Miz Stanton scoffs. "Not at all!" She says representatives and senators get their jobs on male votes alone. Women don't vote for anyone, and I know Ma's never voted. Miz Stanton shouts across the room, asking her friends if they've ever voted for a congressman or cast a ballot for a judge or even a constable. They all shake their heads.

"Neither have I. So how can he represent my views and opinions on what laws I want passed? Or whether I want to go to war with Mexico or the Indians? Nobody asks me!" Miz Stanton shouts angrily.

The silence in the room is church-like: heavy on awe, short on joy.

Lucy looks green as pond scum. "I can't stand to listen anymore."

"There is so much more, dear," Miz Stanton says gravely. "We ladies will commence the battle, but it will be up to you and Tess to win it."

"Hey, I'll fight!" I grin. Slumped in her chair, Lucy doesn't look like a warrior.

Miz Stanton eyes her warily. "Oh, dear, Lucy, I hope I haven't given you the impression I absolutely detest married life. I dearly love my children. But, along with raising a family, I wanted to do something more with my existence."

"Like have a job?" I ask. "Something exciting and far from home?"

"Absolutely! But what exciting job is open to me? Teacher? Domestic? Cook? Seamstress? What other thrilling jobs are women allowed to hold?" she calls across the room.

"You would make a good lecturer," Miz Mott answers. The women laugh.

Miz Stanton says unless a woman's a Quaker, heaven forbid if she speaks before a mixed group of men and women. Men call those "promiscuous audiences," Miz Stanton says, and she laughs in a way that isn't funny.

"Which brings us back to our problem," Miz Mott says, walking over to our table. "Who will we get to lead our convention?"

"You lead it Miz Stanton," I say. "You're a fiery gal. You'll get the audience on your side." She shrugs and ducks her head shyly. Lucy suddenly comes to life.

"What would you have become, if you could, Mrs. Stanton?" Her voice is clogged with tears. Cripes, mad one minute, bawling the next. What a ninny.

"Truthfully, Lucy, there is little choice of employment for even the rare, fortunate, educated woman. Men monopolize all the most profitable jobs."

Lucy wilts like a flower on a broken stem. Miz Harrington says a woman teacher earns less than a male teacher, whether he has a brain or not. I can't believe she makes half what her brother does, and he's been teaching four years less.

Miz Stanton has a fit when Lucy sidles up and whispers that old man Manning wants her to be a governess to some younger cousins. She calls it a waste and says Lucy's a smart girl who can go places. She says Abner Manning has built a box around his daughter, won't educate her and now he wants to ship her off to become someone else's responsibility. Miz Manning's face gets red.

"He thinks college for me is a waste of money." Lucy ignores her ma's scowl. Miz Manning heads for the door with an armload of flyers.

"A waste of money," Miz Stanton repeats, drawing out each word. "I suppose she is also a waste of food. A waste of shelter. A waste of clothing. A waste of time."

"Lucy!" With a grouchy grunt, the little fox follows her ma out the door.

When I catch up to them, Miss Priss doesn't hide one bit that she hates me tagging along. Maybe it has something to do with my bare feet. Or that I'm wearing Coop's overalls cut above my ankles with a good stretch of leg hanging out. Priss is gussied up in some starched lily white thing, never mind the sweat pouring off us from the sun beating down our backs. Her straw hat has a long, yellow ribbon dangling to her waist. A sissy hat. I wear one, too, but it's a floppy canal cook's topper Beau tossed me the last time he docked. Priss stares like I've tied a pig to the top of my head.

Yeah, she's dang mad I'm along. Her ma is more cordial, but Priss looks right down her nose and doesn't say a word to me the whole time we traipse the village streets handing flyers to women who answer their doors.

"What's this all about, Miranda?" one lady asks. "I've heard rumors. Something about women working and voting?" Miz Manning explains the conference, but the words come out choked and jerky, like she isn't sure of it herself. She mumbles she's only doing this to help a neighbor.

I know she regrets the favor when some women get nasty. "Miranda, what are you getting mixed up in?" the banker's wife barks. "You have a good life. Why spoil it?" I can see the point. Miz Manning's been cheated out of her inheritance, but still has it made.

But Priss steams like a hot teakettle. "Ignorant, lazy women. Aren't they tired of hanging around the kitchen baking muffin after muffin after muffin?" How many muffins have you baked, honey? Not nearly as many as Beany.

The butcher's wife comes to the door carrying a red-faced, squalling brat and dragging another kid stuck to her leg. Must be the nanny's day off. The sorry woman stares at the paper Miz Manning hands her.

"Can't read," she shouts above the racket.

"Oh, I'm so sorry. Please, let me...I'll read it for you. 'There...there will be a meeting Wednesday and Thursday, July 19 and 20, at Wesleyan Chapel to discuss woman's rights'," Miz Manning stammers above the baby's wails. The butcher's wife stares, dull-faced.

"What rights?" she asks. There's a loud crash and another kid sends up a squawk. Snatching the paper and clutching her kids, the woman backs clumsily into her house. Miz Manning stares after her through the open door then shakes herself like a startled cat, steps quickly down the sidewalk and up to the next house.

"We must get this message to as many women as we can," she says, shaky but determined.

CHAPTER ELEVEN

"Miz Harrington says Frederick Douglass is gonna talk at that conference tomorrow, for sure." Beany hands August a basket of cornbread. I sit at the kitchen table, playing with potato peels.

"Who?" August asks, just before hitting the swinging door with her hip and hustling into the dining room. Laughter drifts into the kitchen from the upstairs wash room. I brace myself for the stampede.

"Frederick Douglass!" Beany says, when August swings back into the hot kitchen. "The most famous colored man in this country, Mama. I told you about him!" So, Beany's up on the news.

"What he doing?" August lifts two heavy pitchers of milk. "Bring that butter, honey, and that bowl of beans." They set their burdens in the dining room and make it back to the kitchen as the mill girls clatter down the stairs. Yakkity-yak-yak.

"He's talking at that conference, Mama. I told you. And don't you hear Miz Harrington talk about it day and night like it's the Second Coming?" Beany's so serious. I laugh.

"Don't blaspheme, girl!" August drops into a chair and fans her face with her wet bandana.

"It's the truth. This woman's rights conference is important. The first of its kind in the whole world. Even Miz Manning and her girl were pacing the streets passing out papers about it."

August stops fanning. "How you know that?"

"Tessie told me. She was with them." Beany looks at me for support.

"Yeah, we handed those papers to every person we saw." I flick potato peels one by one off the pile on the tabletop. "Men even, but most of them threw them on the ground. Some crumpled them up first, then threw them down, then stomped on them." I laugh remembering their angry faces.

"I think I saw some of them papers," August says, rubbing her eyes. "Mr. Riley find a pile on the foyer table and throw them in the burn barrel. Say he don't want Miz Riley joining no woman's gang."

I scatter the peelings in one swoop. "Ma should go to this conference. She could use a few rights, the way he treats her."

Beany looks at August collapsed in the chair with barely enough energy to fan herself. "You should go, too, Mama."

"Ha! Woman's rights for white women not colored women."

"Women are women, Mama. They're talking about all women when they planned this meeting. Right, Tessie?"

"Yeah, I guess."

"How you know that?" August dips her bandana into a glass of water.

"That's what Miz Harrington said. She's in the thick of it."

"You stop snooping around white woman things. You get in trouble."

The buzzer rings. Beany hurries to the dining room and comes back quickly. "Where's that strawberry jam? Your pa's asking for it. Always got to have something not on the table."

"Stop complaining. Here it is, honey."

Beany returns. "They're asking for you, Tessie."

I dismiss dinner with a wave. I can't stand that yakking. All those mill girls talk about is boys, boys, boys. I like eating with Beany and August in the kitchen.

"So, are you going to the convention, Mama?"

August drops her sweaty forehead into the palm of her hand. "White women plan for themselves. Not for colored women. You see a woman of color at that meeting Miz Harrington have in the parlor the other day?"

Beany shakes her head.

"Why not?"

Beany shrugs. "I don't think they know any colored women."

August laughs. "Miz Harrington know me."

"Yeah...."

"Why don't she ask me to help plan her meeting? Don't she think I need woman's rights?"

"Mama, your rights are taken up in abolition."

"*Abolition*? Don't let that fool you. If slavery abolished, it be the colored man get the few rights white man gonna hand out. Colored woman won't get nothin'."

"That ain't true!"

"Yeah, it is." August spreads her hands on the table "There a pecking order in this world, honey, just like in the chicken yard. Today, white man the top rooster. White woman his favorite hen. The slaves, they the chicks scrapping around for crumbs. If slavery outlawed, white man still be king rooster. White woman still get her pick of the corn. Maybe the farmer throw a little bit at the colored man, who knows? But colored woman? She last. She the scrawniest hen in the yard. She scrapping for what's left and it ain't much."

That mad buzzer rings again. Beany throws a worried glance over her shoulder and hurries to the dining room.

CHAPTER TWELVE

"Stop dragging your tail, Beany."

"I don't wanna go!"

She snatches at the doorjamb. "It's too hot for all this walking."

"What walking? Your feet can't carry you across the street?" I grab her dress to pull her off the porch and tear the waist, just a little.

"You ripped my dress!"

"Shut up, cry baby! Twenty girls wore this rag before you. Who do you think you are, a princess?" I grip her mop top.

"Ow!"

"Hush up and move!" I steer her down the front steps. Lordy! All her yapping trying to get her ma to Miz Stanton's conference, and now I have to pull her across the street like a pig to slaughter.

"I don't wanna go." Beany's brown saucer eyes blink back tears.

"Don't you want to see Frederick Douglass? A famous colored man? Ain't too many of those around." I look up and down the street. "Cripes! Where are all these women coming from?"

Wagonloads of women parade from every direction down Fall Street toward the chapel. Wagonloads of farm women. Carriage after carriage of village women. My mouth flaps open with surprise. From the reception Miz Manning got passing out flyers, I didn't think anybody would take up Miz Stanton's offer to explain them their rights. But women stand at every crossroad. I don't recognize half of them. They must be coming from all over the county—maybe even farther.

"Thank goodness, you've made it." A large lady waves at two women just walking up.

"We came by train," the one with the pink hat replies. "Had arranged ahead for a carriage to take us from the train to the chapel..." She stops to catch her breath and her companion finishes the sentence. "...but we had to walk from the station because all the carriages were taken." They fan themselves with dusty gloves.

Lizzie Stanton's meeting is quite a party! And look! Here's the round, red butcher's wife. Without her squawking brats.

"Charlotte!"

I twist in the direction of a familiar squeal. Miss Priss—all gussied up—waves a hanky. She and her ma are in the Stanton carriage, Lucy flapping her hand at a young gal walking down Fall Street. Miz Stanton slows her horse in front of the chapel.

"Look, Bean."

"I see her."

"The princess arrives at the ball." I snort. "You ready?"

"No."

"Come on! You heard Miz Harrington. This is a history-making event. You want to be part of history, don't you?"

"Maybe, but history don't want to be part of me."

I clamp my hand on Beany's wrist. "Get ready! We're crossing."

"Those horses gonna stomp us!"

"Shut up, sissy!"

We dash across the street, coughing on dust. I keep my grip on Beany's wrist. First chance she gets, the kid will scramble back home to practice penmanship.

The sidewalk in front of the chapel is stuffed with hot, sweating women, and I fight not to be pushed back into the street. "Look at this! It's like a parade."

"Don't hear no band."

"Okay, smarty, it's a...what do they call that parade in church?"

"How do I know?"

"A...a...a procession! That's what it is. A procession for woman's rights."

Jammed in the crowd, I twist my neck around. "Men! What they doing at a woman's rights conference? Prob'ly spying." I grin and nudge Beany's ribs. The excitement makes me giddy and I feel like shouting.

"Church door's locked!" someone yells.

Miz Stanton bustles up, ready to take charge. I push Beany closer to the front.

"Boy! You there," Miz Stanton calls. "Crawl through the window and open the door for us, please."

The kid scrambles in, unlocks the heavy door, the crowd pushes into the chapel and women begin elbowing each other for seats. The men come right in, too, and I swear that flyer said gents could only come the second day.

I sink down on the floor near the front, pulling Beany with me. We lean into the shadows and I feel Beany relax. I know she's worried about being in the white folks' church.

Pretty soon an old guy comes out and says he's James Mott, chairman of the convention. I snort. Great start! A second fellow says he's Thomas M'Clintock and they're gonna let his wife, Mary Ann, be secretary—sure, the job with all the work and he'll get all the credit.

Next, Mott introduces his wife, Lucretia, who prattles on about the convention's purpose—which I thought everybody already knew, or why else were they here? Now comes Miz Stanton. She fidgets and rustles her papers—a lot more nervous than when she's preaching in her parlor—but then she gets down to business. By the time she pulls out her Declaration she's almost chatty. She talks about how men have wronged women since the beginning of time, keeping them from working and taking their money. How women can't be doctors and lawyers—a plug for Miss Priss. How women are trapped home with the kids all day, loaded down with cooking, washing and cleaning up baby messes. She goes on and on and on and the women around me nod their heads and some get teary eyed and *shake* their heads and *hang* their heads. It's a good chance to get miserable.

Miz Stanton ends by accusing men of destroying women's confidence in their abilities, destroying their self-respect and convincing them to be dependent. Women are citizens of this country, she declares, but they have none of the rights and privileges men citizens have. And she is demanding those rights and privileges right now!

The applause dies down and the audience files out of the chapel, most of the women smiling and acting pretty happy for just hearing how downright awful their lives are. I let go of Beany, and she rushes for the door.

Miz Manning and Miss Priss tip-toe up the aisle in front of me neither one turning to say howdy. As we walk through the doorway into the hot sun a harsh voice shouts, "Miranda!"

Abner Manning stands just outside the door. His wife and daughter's faces turn white as flour as they walk slowly toward him. Some women leaving the chapel stare and others glance around warily, looking for their own men, I guess. I walk past and lean against the chapel wall.

"Last night I forbid you to come here!" Manning puffs huge with anger. Lucy and her ma huddle before him, eyes on the ground. "Parading around the streets. Associating with rabble!"

Miz Manning's head flies up. "Elizabeth Cady Stanton is not rabble!" The insult to her friend lights a spark in Miz Manning, but Lucy fizzles. Always mouthy around me, she cows before her old man's bluster.

"Are you just one of many sheep?" Manning accuses. "Nosing your daughter along before you? Embarrassing me!"

"I'm sorry you are embarrassed by our participation, but it's a worthy cause. Woman's rights..."

"Don't talk to me about woman's rights! Get in the carriage." He grabs each of them by an elbow and steers them across the street to their Dearborn. I follow a few steps behind and nobody notices.

"As my wife, you have a right to live in a large, modern home. You have a right to dote on your three, healthy children. You have the right to purchase fashionable clothes and eat good food." Miz Manning walks with her head up, but Lucy's shoulders shake. Is she angry or afraid? Women move out of their way, as Manning pushes them through the crowd.

"You have the right to order your servants around the house and grounds—yet despite their availability, you insist on groveling in those filthy gardens! I allow you to visit your relatives any time you wish. What rights are you talking about?"

There's a short silence. "I have everything I need, Abner. But I want more for Lucy. You know that."

Manning boosts them into the carriage. "Lucy! All I ever hear from you is '*Lucy*!' She'll have just as good a life as you do! How many times must I repeat? I will take care of her." He climbs in after them.

Fall Street teams with walkers and Manning's driver can barely urge the horse into the flow. I'm able to stick to the side of the carriage just below a window and hear everything the big bug says.

"She doesn't need to be taken care of, Abner! Don't talk about her like she's an invalid!" I grin. That's it, lady! Show some spunk.

"I've said it over and over, Miranda, she will not suffer."

"She's suffering already. Her opportunities are limited and she knows it."

"Opportunities for *what*?" I hate his scornful tone, and he's not even my old man. I feel a small twinge of sympathy for Miss Priss.

Finally, Lucy speaks. "I have goals, Father. Dreams. Aspirations."

"You have your head in the clouds! You're worse than Jeremy. You were born female. Swallow it! But you won't if your mother keeps encouraging your outrageous *goals*, *dreams* and *aspirations*." I hear loud sucking sounds and a thick stream of smoke shoots out the carriage window above my head. The crowd thins as we cross the bridge over the canal.

"Jeremy is going to college, then Freeman," he says with fake patience. He blows out another stream of smoke. How thoughtful not to suffocate them. "They have to earn a living to support families. Lucy will find a husband. That is if you don't poison her mind with silly notions of a better life as—God help her—a lawyer!" His laugh is crusty, cruel. "You just don't see how preposterous that is."

It's silent inside the carriage, but I stick to the side, not wanting to miss anything. I have a feeling something's gonna blow.

"I should have known Elizabeth Stanton would be one of the trouble-makers," Manning growls.

"I admit Lizzie makes me nervous." There's a catch in Miz Manning's voice that bodes trouble.

"She makes me furious!"

"But when I hear the disdain in your voice over something meant to improve the treatment of your female child—that intelligent, striving girl sitting right here..." There's that catch again, that painful twitch. "...it makes me want to join with my whole heart and soul in this crusade for woman's rights!"

There's a hacking and coughing as Manning chokes on cigar smoke. Cripes! I never expected a speech like that from Lucy's ma. Guess her old man didn't either. Sounds like he's barking out his guts. The driver clicks the reins, the black horse breaks into a trot and I jog alongside. Manning wheezes and tosses the cigar out the window. There's a long silence before his wife speaks.

"I'm going to the conference tomorrow. Lucy is going with me."

"Go! Go to your damn *woman's rights* conference!" Manning pounds the carriage door once with his fist. I fall back and watch the Dearborn turn down Washington Street.

CHAPTER THIRTEEN

I drag Beany back the second day because Frederick Douglass is gonna talk. Nobody stops Beany from coming in, and we sit up front against the wall again. Today, I'm hoping for a little more excitement. Had enough drowning in self-pity yesterday. I see Miz Manning and Lucy in a middle row. Miz Manning's jaw is set, arms crossed. When I glance back a minute later, they hang limp at her sides. She looks like she's made a mistake and is hoping to fix it. Then I see Lucy's arm linked through her ma's, anchoring her down.

"Yesterday Mrs. Stanton read the Declaration of Sentiments," Lucretia Mott says from the stage. "Today, we will vote on them."

Miz Stanton gets up and reads the Declaration again, then starts in on the Resolutions, a bunch of numbered demands the women are making on men to improve women's lives. Miz Stanton's resolutions say laws that hold women back—like the ones that won't let them into the same colleges men go to—are bad and should be abolished. She says women have every right to go to good schools and end up with good jobs. Right now, a woman can't be much more than a teacher. That's the highest she can go.

Miz Stanton says married women should be allowed to keep the money they earn in those little piddling jobs men let them have, and not have to turn it over to any man who sticks out his hand. She pretty much says women are just as smart, good, ambitious and holy as men, and it's high time they got credit for it. Everybody agrees, and all the resolutions she reads pass, 'til she gets to Resolution No. 9 and then all hell breaks loose.

When she demands that women vote, some gals start whining, "No, no, we can't do that. We don't want to vote. We can't vote." Like a bunch of squalling 'fraidy cats. Even some women who helped her organize the convention—Miz Mott and Miz M'Clintock—say they think women voting is outrageous. I'm flummoxed because these women have been voting on these resolutions all morning like it's perfectly normal. What's so different about casting a ballot to elect the president?

"Oh, Lizzie, thou will make us ridiculous!" Miz Mott moans from the stage where she and the other big bugs sit. "We must go slowly."

But good old Lizzie barrels right on. Won't back down. "If we can vote, ladies," she shouts loud and clear, "we can win our other goals much more quickly." Some women yell support. Others boo her to sit down.

Then Frederick Douglass stands up and the hoots and catcalls stop. Douglass walks to the podium and the chapel falls silent. I wonder how white folks will take to being lectured by a colored man. Miz Mott's husband introduces Douglass and the audience claps politely, but still more than they clapped for Lizzie Stanton after that No. 9 thing.

Douglass wastes no time. "I absolutely support, without reservation, Mrs. Stanton's voting resolution," he begins in a deep voice. "The right to vote is the absolute basis for freedom and equality, and I am a firm believer in freedom—and equality. For myself. For my black brothers and sisters suffering in the shackles of slavery. *And for women.*" Miz Stanton's supporters in the front rows hum their approval.

"Women are not free, ladies and gentlemen. They are not equal to men. God created them equal, but men do not treat them as equal. Owning human beings is physical, mental and emotional captivity. The slavery imposed upon women is mental and emotional, and, yes, at times, physical, too."

Douglass speaks calmly, sounds smart, but damn is he scary looking. His dark hair is long, kinky and sticks straight out from his head. He isn't very old, but he has a streak of white hair shooting straight back from above his right eyebrow. He has a black-bearded chin and a mustache, and if he wasn't dressed up in a white man's suit of clothes, I doubt anyone would have let him in.

"I have come to lend my assistance to this first woman's rights convention, because I am a firm believer in woman's rights as part of the freedom of all people."

"The vote equals power, ladies!" Miz Stanton shouts. "Once women can vote, equal education, equal employment, equal opportunity will follow!"

"That is absolutely ridiculous," shouts old man Thacker, the banker. He heaves his big belly up in the row behind Miz Manning, bumping into Lucy who turns and glares at him. "Women can't make decisions. Oh, little ones around the house, maybe, but not difficult and intelligent decisions about where the country is going."

I shout my disagreement, but nobody hears me. They're all shouting louder.

"Why can't they, Mr. Thacker?" Miz Stanton challenges, waving to her supporters to pipe down.

"They don't have the mental equipment," he grumbles to a chorus of boos from the front row. "And besides, their place is in the home," he barks before sitting down to more boos. His pet wife chimes in that women have more important things to think about than laws and politics.

"Like dinner and diapers?" Miz Stanton quips. "Solving those problems takes very little thought."

The scrawny-necked minister from across town says God made woman mild and dependent for her own protection and gets the crowd yelling when he says it's crude of Miz Stanton and the other women to speak in public and in front of a mixed audience of men and women. "Your promiscuous behavior is insulting to every good woman in Seneca Falls! Your husband should not have allowed it!"

"My husband does not own me!" Elizabeth Cady Stanton roars and the crowd shuts pan.

I nudge Beany, who eyeballs Miz Stanton like she's a wildcat in a hen house. "Hey, Bean, I heard her husband left town over this voting thing." I chuckle to myself. Voting must not be included in Henry Stanton's version of the equality of women.

"The law says he does," the minister replies, tugging at his shirt collar. "The law and almighty God! God created woman inferior for a reason, and gave her man as her master and protector!"

"Superstition! Fear! That's all it is!" Miz Stanton shoots back. "Control of one half of the human race by the other. I do not believe God wants half his creatures to be dominated by the other half! If so, why bother creating them?"

Thacker's wife pats her husband's arm and says man needs a helpmate.

"A helpmate, yes. A slave, no!" Douglass booms.

When a wispy-voiced female sings out that women are the frailer sex, Miz Stanton laughs—a raunchy chortle that reminds me of my canal buddy Beau. "If women can scrub floors, lift huge cooking pots and carry heavy babies," she shouts back, "they can muster the strength to fill out a paper ballot and drop it in a box!"

Shouts of "Hoorah!" and "Amen!" shake the chapel. More gals jump to Miz Stanton's side.

"If men are so much stronger than women, why don't they stand over the washboard and do the laundry?" Lizzie bellows, egged on by the cheers.

The men on stage try to get control of the meeting, while their wives try to calm down wildcat Lizzie. Insults fly back and forth. Some get brave and join Miz Stanton and Douglass, speaking out in favor of the female vote. Others come up with a slew of lame reasons why women wouldn't, couldn't and shouldn't.

Someone begs the crowd not to tax a woman's brain with laws and politics. Someone else charges the family will fall apart if a woman is given a man's rights. Another churchy type shrieks, "It's immoral!"

Finally, Miz Stanton dismisses her opponents with a flick of her hand, takes a vote and the resolution passes, just barely. Lizzie looks relieved— and dang proud.

"Now come forward, ladies, and place your signatures on these powerful documents. Launch this new era for women!" Miz Stanton urges the audience forward with a wave of her arm, but not everyone steps up.

The Motts, M'Clintocks and Hunts all sign. And Miz Stanton, of course, slaps her name down. Miz Manning does not. I watch Lucy nudge her ma and point at the table where a long line of women and a few men wait to scratch the paper with a quill. I see Lucy's friend, Charlotte, walk up and sign her name.

"You've gone too far, Elizabeth," a crabby hag snarls, pushing through the chapel door. "This is definitely not what I expected."

"What did you expect, dear? Lace-making lessons?" Miz Stanton chirps, like she's the only bird with the worm.

I let go of Beany's arm and she races for the door. I work my way past the nosy women who won't sign the Declaration but hang around to snoop on those who do.

Miz Stanton tells Miz Mott they must have a second convention soon. Two weeks from now in Rochester, and the Quaker lady laughs. "Elizabeth, we're not even out the door."

I stretch toward the signing table and strain to see the names of women brave enough to take a stand for woman's rights. Nope, Miz Manning's isn't there. And after all the work she did passing out those flyers.

CHAPTER FOURTEEN

I did more than sort flyers at Miz Stanton's house in the days before the convention. I kept her three little boys out of her hair. It was fun kicking balls, climbing trees and throwing stones in the river. I took a real shine to Neal, Kit and Gat, and I'm lucky—Miz Stanton took a shine to me, too. Today she asks me back on a paying basis to watch the tykes while she cleans and cooks, although I notice she's spending a lot of time reading newspapers and writing letters.

And being at the Stantons gives me a chance to spy on the Mannings next door, who, I admit, have a grand old house. It isn't as large as our boarding house, but it has tall, wide oak doors with long, oval windows instead of solid planks. A brick path lined with red and yellow roses winds up to a wraparound porch dressed with white wicker furniture and fussy green ferns. Miz Stanton says Miz Manning pampers—that's her word—the house with needlepoint pillows and lace doilies. As I chase the Stanton boys around the side yard, I smell flowers—the scent coming from inside the Manning house—and see bright blooms hanging on green stalks that stick like swords out of glass vases perched on tables and window sills. None of that frill would survive in the Stanton house. I also see a little boy running from window to window watching the Stanton kids chase and whack each other as they gallop around in the fresh air.

I'm on the front porch, setting rules for tag, when Miz Manning and Lucy—stiff and glum—walk up the sidewalk. On Thursday, Miss Priss left the convention angry and I figured it had a lot to do with Miz Manning sitting like a goose stuck in tar when Miz Stanton invited the audience to sign her Declaration of Sentiments. Lucy stomped out in a royal snit after her pains to push and pull her ma to the signing table didn't pan out.

Neal Stanton tries to yank Kit off the porch and they start swinging at each other.

"No hitting or we won't play." That's one of Miz Stanton's rules. I feel obliged to respect it, since she's paying me real money to watch her brats, but I intend to teach these ruffians some mean fisticuffs, maybe out behind the barn.

"Good afternoon, Tess." Miz Manning stops at the foot of the steps.

"Afternoon, ma'am."

"I understand you're a big help to Mrs. Stanton"

I smile. "She hired me to keep these boys in line, so she can get some work done."

"Oh, is she busy?"

I laugh. "Well, she said she had pies to bake, but she's been in there reading newspapers, since I got here an hour ago. You go on in, though. She'll tell you the convention buzz that's got her giddy as a goose."

Lucy rolls her eyes and stalks past me. Her ma knocks on the door, and Miz Stanton calls a cheery, "Come in!"

I find a few tin cans under the porch and hand them to the boys. "Dig some worms and we'll go fishing. And keep an eye on your little brother." Gat is two years old and determined to keep up.

"You coming?" Neal grabs the biggest can away from Kit.

"In a minute. You go on down to the garden. And be careful not to dig up the tomatoes. Your ma'll be mad, and I won't be able to take you any-where."

They leave dragging Gat. I lean against the screened front door. The women are in the dining room, where Miz Stanton has dozens of newspa-pers spread out on the table.

"Listen to this!" Miz Stanton says. "'The most shocking and unnat-ural incident ever recorded in the history of womanity'."

Womanity? I don't have much schooling, but that doesn't sound like a word to me.

Miz Stanton laughs like a teamster. "Here's another one. 'Unwomanly behavior...no doubt at the expense of their more appropriate duties'," she reads with a haughty huff. "This one says equal rights will 'demoralize and degrade' women, and 'prove a monstrous injury to all mankind'. I swear, Miranda, we couldn't have done a better publicity job ourselves! This is just what I want. Better! All this fuming and fussing over a few hundred women getting together in a church to demand to be treated like human beings! You'd think we were plotting to overthrow the government!"

"Well, this one does call it 'a petticoat rebellion arranged by love-starved spinsters'." I hear the smile in Miz Manning's voice. I feel sorry for her after that tongue-lashing her husband gave her.

"They call us *Amazons*," Miz Stanton says. "I *like* that! And they say the notion that men and women are created equal is preposterous. Yes, this is just the publicity we need for our second convention in Rochester. You are coming, Miranda." It isn't a question.

I hear Miz Manning's loud sigh. "No, Elizabeth, I'm not. Abner won't allow it." I see Lucy, leaning against the doorjamb between the dining room and foyer, hang her head.

"Miranda!" Miz Stanton looks up from her newspaper. "Now I know he browbeat you into not signing the Declaration."

"How did you...?"

"It was obvious! All the intelligent women signed...except you. How did he threaten you?"

"I...I can't talk about it, Lizzie." She glances at Lucy.

"Well, I can see Lucy's angry. Really, I don't blame her." Miz Stanton rustles through a stack of newspapers.

"It's more regret!" Miss Priss pushes away from the doorjamb. "You've missed an opportunity, Mother, never to be recovered. To have your name—Miranda Manning—on a document that will go down in history!"

"That chance is gone. Lucy's right—a lost opportunity. And this one by your own making, Miranda."

"Oh, Lizzie, you don't understand."

"Explain it to me.

"Not now."

"When...?"

"Please!" Miz Manning glances again at pouting Priss.

Miz Stanton sighs loudly. "Fine. But surely he can't prevent you from traveling to Rochester."

Miz Manning slumps into a chair.

"You'll come with me. He has no reason to fear for your safety, if that's his problem."

"No, it's not that."

"Tell him you're visiting relatives."

"No! I'm sorry, Elizabeth. Please, I can't talk now,' There's a hitch in Miz Manning's voice that snags Miz Stanton's attention, and she calms right down.

"Oh. Oh, yes. Well. We'll talk later, dear."

I cross the porch and squat near the open dining room window. I hear Miz Stanton shifting newspapers.

"Read to us, Lucy. What else do those male writers say about our wonderful convention?"

Lucy shakes out and folds a section of newspaper. "This is from the front section of the *Philadelphia Public Ledger and Daily Transcript*."

She clears her voice like she's some great speechmaker. "A woman is nobody. A wife is everything. A pretty girl is equal to ten thousand men, and a mother is, next to God, all powerful...The ladies of Philadelphia, therefore...are resolved to maintain their rights as Wives, Belles, Virgins, and Mothers, and not as Women."

"And not as women? Outrageous!" Miz Stanton stomps her feet, one-two-three—"*not-as-women.*" I peek over the window sill and see her doubled over laughing. "Wives, belles, virgins and mothers—what are they but women? Since this drivel wasn't written by the wives, belles, virgins and mothers of Philadelphia—but instead by husbands, dandies, lechers and fathers who pass judgment under the guise of stodgy male editors—I think it's a bunch of poppycock!"

I lean just far enough to see her lay a plump hand on Miz Manning's arm and pat it gently.

CHAPTER FIFTEEN

"Tell me again about that Frederick Douglass." August fans herself with the end of a damp towel.

As it turns out—to my surprise—she isn't mad Beany crossed the street to the chapel two days in a row. Actually says she's glad Beany got to see a famous colored man. Is glad those white folks let her in. We sit on the back porch a couple days after the convention, catching a breeze, after Beany and August sweat themselves slick washing supper dishes.

"Miz Harrington still bragging how Mr. Douglass stood up for the women voting," August says, an odd touch of pride in her voice. "And it two weeks past." August minds her own business, but she doesn't miss much.

"Yeah, he got right up and talked. Not afraid one bit." I whittle a stick with the new pocket knife I bought with money from Miz Stanton. The door from the dining room swings and someone walks into the kitchen.

"And he's smart, Mama. And dressed nice. Like a white man. Black suit of clothes. Clean. Hair kind of wild, though." So Beany took it all in, huh. "But I like Miz Stanton better." Beany never said a word to me about liking Miz Stanton.

"I remember how she rile that church lady at that temperance meeting." August laughs. "Me in the kitchen and hear that ol' hen cackle!"

"She's quick with her tongue!" Beany says. "You should have heard her sass the banker and even the minister. She ain't afraid. She and Frederick Douglass, they stood together on the voting. Said after women get the vote, they can vote themselves in all sorts of other freedoms."

The door swings again. Maybe a hungry mill girl sneaking leftovers. We sit quiet, listening to crickets.

"So, the white woman gonna get some rights." August chuckles and pokes a finger in Beany's belly.

"All women, Mama."

"Yeah, you say." She stands up. "I'm gonna wet this towel. Cool me down some. Ain't this a hot night!"

Through the open kitchen door, I hear the pump splash cold water into the sink. Then it squeaks to a stop and August says something, real low. When she doesn't come back outside, Beany goes to the door. I see her back tense and her fists grab the sides of her dress. I get up fast and peek through the doorway. Pa has his arms around August and is straining on tip-toe to nuzzle her neck. August is straining in the opposite direction. Beany starts to quiver like a wire strung too tight.

August glances over her shoulder. "Mr. Riley, it real hot. Let me go out on the porch. My Beany waiting for me. Look, she right there by the door. Tessie, too."

"Get the hell out of here!" Pa shouts over his shoulder.

We don't move. I smell booze every time he twitches.

Pa rubs his stubbly cheek against August's face. She tries to pull away, but he pins her arms behind her.

"Don't fight me, black August." He grips her wrists with one hand, puts the other on her breast and pushes her with his pot belly against the sink.

"Pa! Leave her alone!" I see the iron fry pan on the sink, still wet from washing.

"Get the hell out!"

"Leave my Mama alone!" Beany shoots through the doorway like a stone from a slingshot, grabs his arm and tries to pull him off. I'm so shocked, I can't move.

"Beany, no!" August pulls one arm free and pushes Pa's hand away from her breast.

Pa slaps at Beany then pushes her hard. "GET!" She bounces against the wall and falls on the floor.

"Stop it, Pa!" I grab his shirt at the neck and try to yank him off August. I hate him for doing this. Hate him even more for doing it in front of me.

"Please, Mr. Riley," August gasps, jammed against the sink.

Beany jumps up and comes at him again. "Let her go you stupid drunk!"

"Beany, no!" August exclaims, shocked. She tries to twist away.

"I said don't fight!" Pa growls mean as a tom cat and pulls the arm behind August's back up real quick and she screams. In a flash Beany grabs the fry pan off the sink and slams it down fast and hard on Pa's ugly head. KUNK! He waves in the air like dirty mist, then his hands slip off August and he slumps to the floor.

August slides down against the sink and her arm swings at her side like a piece of meat on a hook. "Oh, no, no." Her face twists in pain. "Beany, what you do? Oh, Lordy, no."

Beany sits down on the floor beside her ma. "Sshhhh, Mama…your arm. Help her, Tessie."

My stomach flip-flops. This is big trouble. Not only is August's arm hurt bad—Beany has knocked Pa clean out.

"It's hanging awful funny." I don't like the wiggle in my voice.

"She needs a doctor."

"Yeah, I know, but…I don't know if he'll come. I don't know if he fixes coloreds."

"Why not?"

I stare at her. "You ever go to the doc for something? When you're sick?"

"Mama fixes us when we're sick."

"See, the doc don't know you. And you're not white, so maybe he won't help you."

"But look at Mama's arm hanging there! I don't know how to fix it. Do you?"

"No."

"Does your ma?"

"Doubt it."

"So Mama needs a doctor, Tessie, do something!"

August tries to hold her hanging arm steady with her good one. I grab a dish towel and tie the arm snug to her chest. Then I stoop down, put my arm around her waist and lift her off the floor. She cries out and sags, her legs rubbery.

"We'll go to Miz Manning's house."

"That's across the canal! Mama can't walk it."

"She's got to. Maybe Miz Manning can get the doc to fix her. She's her cook—sort of—after all."

"But it's a long way."

"Stop whining! You want me to do something, right?"

I half carry, half drag August through the back door, down the steps, across the sloping backyard and toward the bridge. She cries out with every jiggle.

"We won't make it all the way there," Beany wails.

"Shut up and walk!" I know she's scared for her ma and confused about what to do. Maybe she's scared about whacking Pa with that fry pan, too. Confused and scared, just like me.

When we get across the bridge, Beany tries to take August, but she's too little and I take her back. It's a long walk to Washington Street. Halfway to the Manning house, we meet Ma coming home from church.

"Pa hurt August. Real bad."

Ma gives August an odd look. Like she isn't sure what to do or say.

"Ma! Your stinking drunk husband pulled August's arm right out of its socket! We're taking her to the Manning house. Maybe they can get the doc to fix her."

"Oh, August," Ma says finally, her voice teary. She turns and waves at a carriage coming down the road. The driver takes one look at August, slaps the reins on his horse's back and drives on.

No more carriages come by. We walk, taking turns carrying August. When we reach the Manning house, Ma goes up the steps, while we wait on the sidewalk, drenched with sweat.

The housekeeper answers the door. She keeps trying to see past Ma and shakes her head like she doesn't want to let us in, but Ma pushes inside and calls out "Mr. Manning! Mrs. Manning! It's Moira Riley from the boarding house!"

The housekeeper apologizes as her bosses come running, but Ma talks right over her and points to us huddled outside. Manning comes down quickly and helps me bring August into the house. Beany walks right in, and I know tonight she doesn't care if it is a white man's house.

We lay August on a big sofa in a dark room with lots of books. Manning looks at her arm then sends his driver for the doctor. Beany kneels on the floor next to August and strokes her head. When I look back into the foyer, I see three faces watching us. One belongs to Miss Priss. My temper flares. We ain't no circus act! I stride to the doorway.

"Are those colored people?" It's the little boy who spies on the Stanton brothers.

"Yeah." I lean against the doorjamb.

"They're from our boarding house, Freeman," Lucy whispers. Yeah, *your* boarding house.

"Why are they here?"

"The woman is hurt. Father sent for the doctor."

"Doc Wilson won't help a person of color," Jeremy says in the hushed tone of an undertaker. "I heard him say so in the barbershop."

"Doctors take care of everyone. They take an oath." Miss Priss, the know-it-all. But this time I hope she's right.

"A what?' Freeman asks.

"They promise to always help people who are hurt or sick."

"Promises can be broken." Jeremy really is kind of creepy.

Suddenly Miz Manning is next to me. "Quiet children. The woman is badly injured. Her shoulder is dislocated." I hate the way they call her "the woman." Like you'd say, "the chair" or "the carrot."

August has sunk into the depth of Manning's huge brown sofa. She's stopped moaning, but I know she's still full of pain and fear.

"Her name is August. That's her daughter, Beany."

Freeman giggles. Beany looks at him over her shoulder with sad, watery eyes.

"Well, this is not a stage show," Miz Manning says. "Go upstairs."

"Mother, I want to stay," Lucy says quickly. "Please. I feel like I know them and...Tess. And I'm concerned about...about August."

Miz Manning sighs. "Fine. Jeremy, take your brother."

"I want to stay," Freeman whimpers. Heavy footsteps approach the foyer and both boys hurry upstairs.

"I'm allowing Lucy to remain here," Miz Manning tells her husband firmly. "She knows these people from the boarding house and from passing out..." She stops before mentioning the convention. Manning opens his mouth, but snaps it shut at the sound of Doc Wilson's snarl.

"Manning! You brought me down here at nine o'clock at night for a nigger? I don't work on niggers. I told your man that but he wouldn't let me out of the carriage."

Abner Manning draws himself up tall, sticks out his barrel chest. "Doctor Wilson! You will not use that word in this house!"

"I'm not an abolitionist like you, Manning."

"But you are a doctor," Miz Manning says calmly, "and you did take the Hippocratic Oath."

"That's for white people. Not ni...slaves."

"August is not a slave, but you can't refuse to help her for any reason." Anger makes Manning seem even taller, bulkier. Of course, I've never seen him not angry.

"But let me make it easier for you, doctor. That woman with the injured arm is my employee. She's my boarding house cook. She was attacked, mauled, and she needs immediate medical attention or she can't work for me." Manning puts a large arm around Doc Wilson's shoulders and turns him toward the dark room where August lays. "Does that make it easier for you?"

Wilson shakes him off. "I never touched a colored in my life and I don't intend to start now!"

"I will pay you, if that's what you're worried about."

"It's not the money. I just won't do it."

"What's your fee?"

"I don't want your money!"

"I will double your normal fee, and I won't tell your wife I saw a fancy girl sitting on your lap last Tuesday night in Waterloo."

"Tuesday's my poker night." The old doc shifts his eyes around the room.

"You need two hands to play, Wilson, and I only saw one hand on your cards."

Doc Wilson pulls at his skimpy moustache, looks at August like she's a cat with mange, rubs his sharp nose and finally mumbles, "Okay, I'll fix the damn arm."

"And you'll do as good a job as you would if she were white. Right, Wilson? She'll never have a problem with it."

Wilson shakes his head in disgust. "No, she won't. Cut off her shirt."

We stand beside the sofa and watch Miz Manning take scissors to August's sweaty blouse. When August lifts herself to slide the pieces off, Lucy sucks in a chest full of air, her eyes glued to August's scarred back. Thick, wide stripes crisscross from shoulder to shoulder. Old scars that still look wicked. I've seen them before, when I stumbled accidentally into the laundry room while August had a bath.

Doc Wilson starts turning and pulling August's arm. I tell myself any person needing an arm pulled back into its socket would cry as painfully, and that August is not being tortured by hateful, old Wilson. Beany shivers every time August shrieks. She sees Lucy watching and moves behind her ma, blocking the rich girl's view of August's scars and suffering.

A loud gasp from August signals the arm flipping into its socket. Wilson straps her arm to her chest in a firm sling, wipes his hands on his shirt front and says he's finished.

"Lucy," Miz Manning says, "bring a clean blouse of mine from upstairs." Priss returns quickly.

"I didn't know which one, Mother. I brought your oldest, with the torn buttonhole."

"Sshhhh." Miz Manning frowns. She takes the blouse and gently slips a sleeve over August's good arm. Her hands shake as she lays the shirt across August's scarred back.

"This won't do. I should have put it on her before Doctor Wilson taped her arm. Bring my white shawl, Lucy."

"I'll bring it back, Mrs. Manning," Ma says, placing a hand gently on August's drooping head.

"No, she may keep the shawl," Miz Manning replies softly. "And take the blouse for when she can move her arm enough to put it on."

Doc Wilson closes his black bag with a sharp snap. "Pay me and I'm gone." Manning hands him some cash, and Wilson leaves without another word.

Manning and Ma lift August off the couch and move her carefully down the front steps to the Dearborn. Ma climbs into the carriage then guides August onto the seat as Manning lifts her from behind. His wife hands Ma a thin blanket. She lays it across August's lap then cradles her to her shoulder.

"Get in," Manning tells Beany. She scales the steps smoothly and huddles on the floor at August's feet.

"Make it an easy ride, Jim," Manning tells his driver.

There's a shout and Constable Parker jogs up, puffing.

"Mr. Manning," he pants. "I hear somebody at your house was attacked. Your wife?"

"No, my boarding house cook."

"Who did it?"

"Liam Riley. He dislocated her arm. She's in the carriage."

Parker stares up at August's bleak face. "A nigger." He turns to Manning with a crooked grin.

"Don't use that language around me, Constable."

Hands on his wide hips, Parker looks back at August and shakes his head.

"Riley attacked her. Doctor Wilson just set her shoulder."

"Wilson?" Parker laughs. "He'll take a ribbing for that!"

"There are witnesses." The muscles in Manning's broad shoulders twitch.

"Yeah? Who?"

"Me!" I yell. "I saw it. So did Beany." I point into the carriage.

"Kids? Kids saw it?" He smirks.

"What makes them different from any other witnesses, Parker?"

"Well, these witnesses are real different," he says, giving Manning a how-can-you-miss-it look. "I know Tess, here. The town's worst troublemaker. Look at her. Looks like a boy! And that one...that one's—colored! In fact, your so-called victim's just a colored cook."

"So-called victim? She was brutalized!"

"Who cares if a black cook got her arm twisted?" Parker turns to leave.

"I care!" Manning grabs Parker and spins him around. The constable looks down at the hand gripping his arm. Manning is taller, but the constable is heavier, although most of Parker's bulk hangs like corn-filled saddlebags.

"Abner," Miz Manning says quietly. Her husband scowls and releases Parker's arm. I hear a door open and Miz Stanton comes out onto her front porch.

"I voted for you in the last two elections, because I expect you to protect my family and my property," Manning says.

"Oh, your property. Is she your slave?" Parker sneers. I really wish Manning would slug him.

"No! She's my employee and she's been attacked and injured. She can't work. Liam Riley has deprived me of my employee's services. Does that make a difference to you now?"

"Well..."

"I want you to go down to my boarding house...in fact, I'll take you there...and arrest Riley for assault! Here's my carriage. Get in!"

"I ain't riding with no nigger!"

Rage flares in Manning's eyes. His hands flex into fists. His wife breathes another, "*Abner.*"

"All right then, we'll walk." He glances at me. "You want to ride?" I shake my head and glare at Parker, my own hands balled into tight weapons. Manning starts down the sidewalk. After two strides he turns and waits. The lawman spits in the grass, cusses then follows. I stalk a few paces behind like a guard dog. I look back and see Miz Stanton join Miz Manning and Lucy on the grass. They watch us leave, arms gripped across their stomachs. Then it's just Lucy watching as we cross the bridge.

It takes forever getting home. Manning tells his man to drive slowly, but lardbutt Parker, lumbering along like a pregnant cow, slows us to a crawl. When we finally get to the house it's near midnight, but Pa's sitting on the front step with a bucket of beer. Ma's face twitches, a mix of mad and sad.

"Evening, Liam," Parker says.

"Drinking tonight, I see, Mr. Riley." Manning towers over the slouching drunk.

I stop next to the carriage. "It's Saturday night. 'Course he's drinking."

Pa stares up at Manning with bleary eyes. His pants are dirty, his face grizzled with a two-day beard, and his checked vest sports fresh puke.

"Drunk as a skunk. You hurt August, you rat!"

"Hey, hey, girly. That's no way to talk to your pa," Parker scolds. "Now, Liam, tell me what happened here." He crosses his arms and tries to look interested.

"Tess, help us down, please." Ma eases August to the edge of the seat. I reach up but keep one eye on Pa. August moves slowly. It's hard sliding her out of the carriage without jostling her. Her whimpers start fresh tears down Beany's cheeks.

"What happen her?" Pa dips a ladle into the beer bucket. He's so plastered he can't even do his grin and hop routine. I wish Manning would fire him. Throw him out of town. Boot him out of our lives.

Pa catches his breath and belches, shooting a sour stench into the summer air. Ma shakes her head and moves August up the front walk. Beany takes her ma's good arm, kisses her cheek.

"Hey! Where you taking black August?" Pa tries to stand.

"You stay here and talk to the constable," Ma says coldly.

"Naw, I'm going in with black August."

"Riley! Sit!" Manning orders. I wish his bellow had knocked Pa down, but I know it's just the beer.

"Beany..." August calls weakly.

"Take your ma in and come right back," I whisper, holding onto her arm. "You gotta tell Parker what happened." Beany studies the constable like a trapped mouse eyes a hungry cat, but nods.

"So, what happened here, Liam?" Parker asks again. "You pull out your colored cook's arm?"

"Huh?"

"In the kitchen." Manning's voice has a jagged edge that matches the angry lines around his eyes. I wonder if he's worried about August or just mad his property got damaged.

"Naw, I been at Mallory's." Burp. "Came back, fell sleep." He droops against a porch post.

"Constable, this is going nowhere. Arrest him."

"Why?"

"Don't act simple. He committed a crime."

"He says he didn't."

"You have two witnesses who say he did." Manning clenches and unclenches his fists.

"One's a boy-girl, the other's a nigger."

"Parker, you are standing on my property. I'm telling you for the last time to watch your language." Manning takes a deep, steadying breath. "Question the victim then."

"What's the point? She's a...colored, too." I can't believe Parker is this dumb. Manning's scaring me, and I don't scare easy.

"Coloreds can't be trusted to tell the truth."

"Don't give me that malarkey. Do your job!"

Parker tries a weak smile. "Look, Mr. Manning, there's no great damage..."

"A woman was abused! Her arm wrenched from its socket. This drunk did it!"

"Well, there's your answer! He didn't know what he was doing. You can't blame a man for what he does when he's drunk." Parker spreads his hands, like he's explained it all perfectly.

Manning glares at the lawman. The pitch of his voice drops low and menacing. "Yes, I can blame him. I do blame him. Arrest him."

"Got no proof." I wonder if Pa has something on Parker that makes the constable afraid to do his duty. How can Parker be this thick and ignore a big bug like Abner Manning?

"I'm pressing charges against Liam Riley. Arrest him now."

Parker scowls and spits in the grass, but Manning won't let him off the hook. He browbeats the lawman into handcuffing Pa to the porch railing. Then he brings Parker into the house, through the kitchen and into August's hot, narrow room.

Still wrapped in the white shawl, August lays on her skinny cot, damaged goods. Her thin arm looks like a dark twig stuck to her chest. Her neck is red where the sling rubs. Ma sits next to her, wipes her face, talks to her softly, offers her sips of water.

When Manning tells August to tell Parker what happened, she won't say anything. Just thanks him for helping her and begs to be left alone. When Manning insists, August's eyes shift weakly from Ma to Beany.

"No, everything fine, sir. Nothin' happen."

"August, please, tell Constable Parker the truth." Ma's eyes are kind.

August sighs then whispers about being in the kitchen and Pa coming in for a sandwich...

"Mama!"

August gives Beany a quick look and a tiny, sharp head shake.

...and how she slipped on a wet spot on the floor where the pump splashed water...

"Mama!" Louder this time. August gives Beany that fierce look again and Beany shuts pan.

...and how she fell against the sink and popped out her arm. We all stare at the broken woman.

"I don't believe that's what really happened, August," Manning says finally. "You girl, tell Constable Parker what you saw."

Beany stands stiff as a tree trunk near the bedroom door. She looks from Manning to her ma. August stares back with that hard look. That signal.

"Tell Constable Parker what you saw," Manning repeats.

August holds Beany in a powerful eye-lock, but tears start sliding down Beany's cheeks and she breaks away from her ma's forceful gaze, looks straight at Parker and says, "Mr. Riley's always putting his hands on my Mama. Touching her." Each word is a punch. August groans. "Tonight he hid in the kitchen, waiting for her. And when she came in for some water, he grabbed her."

"You see him grab her?" Parker inspects his dirty fingernails.

"I saw his hand on her chest. I saw him kiss her neck. He had her arms pinned behind her back."

Tears flood August's face. I take the rag from Ma, who seems in a trance, and wipe August's eyes and chin.

"Did she let him touch her?" Parker asks with interest.

"She pulled one arm away. Pushed his hand away from her chest."

"Beany, no," August's pleads.

"Then he shouted at her not to fight and snapped her arm up way high and she screamed! And then..."

"I grabbed a fry pan and slugged him with it." I say it fast and loud over Beany's own strong voice.

She pauses, locks eyes with me. Then, "I ain't sorry to tell, Mama." She leans back against the doorjamb, her eyes fixed on Parker's face.

"Wait now. Who hit Mr. Riley?" Parker asks, looking hard and accusing at me, then Beany. Beany's eyes flicker. Her lips open and close.

I take a step forward. "I did. He's lucky I didn't kill him!" If Parker knew Beany hit Pa, my old man's guilt would be wiped out completely in the lawman's eyes. Maybe in Manning's eyes, too.

"Kill your pa? Some daughter you are. When did you come in the kitchen? What'd you see, girly boy?"

"I was in the doorway with Beany. And this isn't the first time he's bothered August."

I watch Ma's hands move like they're fingering a rosary.

"You see him hassle the colored cook tonight?"

"Yes!"

"You see him touch her? Tonight? Put his hands on her, like her pickaninny says?"

"Don't call Beany names!"

"Just tell the constable what happened." Manning crosses his arms and gives me the eyeball.

"He was rough with August, jerked on her arm, and she screamed and I grabbed the fry pan and clobbered him." I shoot a hard look at Beany and she doesn't peep. "I wish I'd killed him!"

"Damn! You're a bad one." Parker shakes his head like it's loose. "If I had a daughter like you, I'd..."

"He deserved it. The drunk's always after August."

Ma pulls out a real rosary and massages the beads. August lays stone-still, eyes closed. Maybe she passed out.

"I'm filing assault charges," Manning says. "Take him to jail."

"I should file charges against that brat." Parker looks to smack me.

"It was a defensive move. Riley's the criminal."

"You're wasting your time. Nobody believes niggers. And that kid ain't reliable. She hates her pa."

"It's the truth and I'll tell it to a judge!" I shout.

Parker cusses hotly, but takes his drinking buddy down to the jail anyway, because Manning walks right behind him all the way.

PART TWO

CHAPTER ONE

It's been almost three years since Pa wrenched August's arm, and he still hates her for getting him hauled off to jail. In his loopy head, the whole thing was her fault. Not that he stayed locked up long. Just overnight. That stink Parker let him out. Never brought him before a judge.

The day after the trouble, Pa dragged himself up onto our front porch, filthy and hung over from his bucket of beer and who knows what else he'd poured down his rotten gullet. Ma stood in the doorway and told him not to come in. He was trouble. She didn't need him. She could run the boarding house herself. But Pa said they were married, and she was his wife, and he had a right to live there with her. He pushed past Ma and fumbled his way through the parlor and dining room and out through the kitchen into the backyard. Why he couldn't just keep going and jump into the canal and drown himself, I don't know.

Abner Manning was mad because Pa got out so quick and took justice into his own hands. He docked Pa's pay for August's doctor bill. Doc Wilson charged Manning top fee for fixing August's arm—ten dollars. "Because he had to touch a nigger" was the barbershop story. Manning paid double, like he promised. Then he took it out of Pa's salary, more than a month's pay, and told him to keep his hands off August or he'd kick him out of this boarding house. Told him to stop drinking. If Manning smelled liquor on him one more time, he was gonna run him out of town. Was Manning really that powerful? And could we really be that lucky?

Pa said, "Yes, sir. Yes sir," while Manning lectured him, but cussed and spit on the sidewalk after the boss' carriage rolled out of sight. The first Saturday after Pa got out of jail, Ma told him, "No drinking. You heard Mr. Manning." He said, "Yeah, yeah," but I heard him mumble, "I'll drink if I want," when Ma turned away.

I think Manning felt sorry for Ma, that's why he didn't fire Pa straight off for boozing like he said when he first took over this dump. Didn't he know Ma would be better off without that drunk? We all would.

Just the other day Pa and me had a mean fight and I yelled, "Get outa here! Nobody wants you." At 16, I'm taller than him now, strong and fast. When he swung at me, I jumped out of his way and taunted him in true canawler style. Lordy, did he cuss. I hooted louder and he cussed more awful. The trouble between me and Pa is getting worse and making everyone miserable. I know the fighting hurts Ma bad. Same thing happened just before Cooper left.

Then this morning, I heard Beany tell August she saw Pa heading toward the barn. Said she sneaked behind him, and he wasn't down in the stables, rooting around for a soft place to nap. Said she heard noise up in my loft and figured Pa was up there looking for money—my pay from Miz Stanton. I lit out to the barn and checked, but it was still in its hiding place. Good thing. It's a nice amount of cash.

Beany is thirteen and showing real spunk. Pa leaves August alone now—maybe he found other women to pester—but sometimes I catch him looking at Beany. She catches him, too, but now when he stares, she stares right back. She's getting bolder. Knows how to stare him down, ignore the flutter in her stomach and not blink.

Yeah, Beany is growing up and sick of the house, but August is tighter with her than ever. A few months back she found a newspaper in the parlor with a drawing of colored folks running through the woods. She brought it into the kitchen where I was making a sandwich and asked Beany to read it to her. I knew right off what kind of paper it was and figured Miz Harrington had left it downstairs. Beany read aloud about a new Fugitive Slave Act. It said slave owners could come up north and take back their slaves who'd run away. August said, "Read that again," so Beany did.

She read that owners didn't even have to come up themselves. They could send slave catchers north to capture the runaways and bring them back south. They got paid good money for this catching—two hundred dollars. Then Beany read about a colored man dragged away from the family he made up here in some little New York town. He'd escaped from a plantation five years ago, and his owner still sent a pack of men to hunt him down with the new law. There'd been a runaway slave law for almost 60 years, but this new tougher law got voted in last September.

August took the newspaper from Beany. Her face hung long. Her mouth pulled down in the corners. Even though she couldn't read, her eyes stared at the paper, but only in one spot, like they were blind or something. Then she said Beany could never go anywhere without her.

"Mama, I got to go somewhere without you. I'm a big girl now." Beany likes to draw the canal boats. She's been writing down Coop's canal tales and drawing pictures to go with them.

"You never go down to the canal with me, Mama. You say you hate it as much as Miz Riley does. How am I gonna draw my pictures, if you don't let me go down there?"

"You stay away from that canal. And don't go uptown neither."

"What if Tess goes with me?" She looked at me for help.

"What help will Tess be?"

"Help for what?" Beany held up her hands, confused.

"Nothin'." August looked miserable. "Just don't go nowhere without me. I mean it."

"You afraid of slave catchers, August?" I peeled an apple with my newest knife.

"I'm afraid of everything. And Beany should be, too."

Later, Beany asked Miz Harrington, "How come slave catchers can come up north? The north's free."

"It's the law."

"What fool made that law?"

"A lot of fools. They're called congressmen."

CHAPTER TWO

Boos and ballyhoos ricochet off buildings like bullets, telling me the Bloomers are coming down Fall Street.

"Hoooooo…it's Halloween!"

"The she-males are out! Scaaa—rrryyyy!"

"Look out! They'll get ya!"

"Booooooooo! Boo—boo—boooooo!"

A gang of young boys, egged on by older beer hall scum, circles two middle-aged women like wolves. The ladies, heads high, eyes straight ahead, inch their way grim-faced toward the mercantile.

What some folks would call a respectable gentleman walks out of the general store, frowns at the women in their short skirts and baggy pants, and lets the door slam shut just as they get there. I run across the street, dodging wagons and horses.

"Hey!" I elbow dirty bodies, land a punch on the biggest loudmouth, grab another by the hair and push him into the pack.

"Scram! Get outa here! Leave 'em alone!" I plant a sharp kick in the butt of the tallest boy—who isn't as tall as me. "Get! Or I'll get savage as a meat axe!" They scatter like cowardly leaves in a bossy wind. I open the door and wave the women inside.

Well, well, guess who's here, back pressed against a pickle barrel? Miss Priss. I see her now and then on the street and when I fetch a Stanton boy playing with her kid brother. She never comes to our boarding house, and we haven't said a word to each other since Pa hurt August. She still hangs around with her mama. Hasn't grown an inch. Still pointy faced. Still has that weird red-yellow hair, but the long bushy tail is gone, twisted up behind her head in a fussy grown-up knot.

The Mannings smile at the two gals I rescued from the mob. Everybody bobs heads and says "Hello" and "Good afternoon," while I grin at the town mothers in pants.

"Thank you, dear." Miz Stanton gives me a shaky smile. "You showed up at just the right moment."

A street rowdy kicks open the door. "Hey, you! Plug ugly!" I ball my fists and light out after him.

"Wait, Tess!" Miz Stanton catches my arm. "He's not worth it."

"Sorry about them hassling you, ma'am. They're just no-account tramps. Like you say, they ain't worth shucks."

Miz Stanton's friend looks me over. "Tess. That's a strong female name. What's the rest of it?"

"You gonna put it in the paper?" I grin at Amelia Bloomer, editor of *The Lily.*

She laughs. "How's this headline? Girl Bops Bloomer Bashers on Fall Street."

I laugh, too, and slap my hands together loudly. "I'm Tess Riley. Live down at the boarding house, backs up on the canal."

"Well, Tess, thank you for rescuing us. I don't know why our choice of attire attracts so much unsavory interest."

I glance at the Mannings. No easy outfits for those gals. All starch and whalebone, both of them.

"Has August's arm healed well?" Miz Manning asks.

"Yeah, she's okay." Been three years and this the first you're asking? "Hey, you gals sure wake snakes with those get-ups."

The women pat their woolen pants, trimmed lacy around their ankles. A shirt tucks into the waist, covered by a long-sleeved, short dress that comes to their knees.

"Look, I'm wearing 'em, too." I spread my legs so Miz Bloomer can see how I split and stitched my skirt. Ma hasn't given up buying me sissy girly clothes, and I haven't stopped fixing them to my taste. "Been wearing these for years. Even before you gals took it up."

I yank off my heavy wool sweater and toss it in a corner, showing off my loose flannel shirt. "Sometimes I go whole hog and just wear my brother's overalls—like when I'm watching your boys, ma'am—but they're getting kinda small on me." That better not be a snicker from Priss if she knows what's good for her.

"Very creative," Miz Bloomer replies. "Look, Elizabeth. We could adapt our long skirts like Tess has. Shorten them even. I love the shorter length. So much easier to get around in." She sticks out her hand. "I'm Amelia Bloomer."

"Yeah, I know." I pump her hand. It's rough, and she has ink under her fingernails. "I read your paper, sometimes. Pretty good stuff."

"Thank you."

"I read that thing you wrote, Miz Stanton. Where you ask, 'What use is all the flummery, puffing and mysterious folding we see in ladies' dresses.' I like that. You're a stitch!"

"Thank you, Tess. I strive to be a stitch. It's much better than a witch, like those young devils make us out to be."

"Are you in school, Tess?" Miz Bloomer asks, stroking a bolt of summer cloth.

"Naw, I'm past that. Too old now, but I didn't go much when I was younger, either. Too much work."

"Oh, you don't like to work?" The newspaper lady eyes me suspiciously.

I hold up my hands. "Hey, don't get me wrong. I ain't lazy. Just picky about how I spend my time. I'd work my butt off on any canal job—driving mules, loading cargo—like my brother. He started as a hoggee, and now he's got a good paying job. I don't shirk from real work, but housework, schoolwork—what's the point? Who needs it?"

Miz Stanton and Miz Bloomer exchange looks. Miss Priss skews up her mouth and turns to face the pickle barrel.

"Now, Tess, that's not exactly true," Miz Stanton says, smiling. "You work hard with my boys. Tess comes twice a week to help me out, Amelia. She's wonderful at inventing games and doesn't mind getting dirty. When Neal and Kit sent Gat out on that raft into the middle of the river, Tess jumped right in and rescued him!"

I can't remember the last time my face turned red from a compliment.

"How old are you, Tess?"

"Sixteen. Like I said, too old for school."

"Do you need money? Besides what Mrs. Stanton pays you, I mean."

"Yeah, sure."

"Well, why don't you work for me? I need a smart girl with spunk."

I was smart enough to know to be careful here. "Doing what?"

"Right now, setting type. Then I'll teach you to run the printing press. Eventually I'd like you to do some reporting."

"Newspaper writing?" I laugh. "You got the wrong gal, Miz Bloomer. I'm not good at that. I mean, I can read and write, but I ain't quick at it."

"But you're bold, Tess. You can be taught to write better. What's valuable is your natural nerve. You've got guts!" I never heard a proper lady use that word before.

"Tess does have courage." I swerve to face Miz Manning. "She wasted no time helping our boarding house cook when her shoulder was injured. Told the constable the whole story. Stood up to her father."

Miss Priss crosses her arms, tucks in her chin and stares at me like a cobra in one of Miz Harrington's science books. Why's your nose in a twist, girly? Because your mama likes me? Don't spit now, sweetie. Remember, you're a lady.

"No one can teach courage, Tess," Miz Bloomer says. "You're a natural. You can start out slowly. Just spend some time at the newspaper office. See how you like it. Lucy's there quite often. She can show you the ropes."

Behind me, the cobra gasps. I laugh, turning to face her. Lucy knows the ropes, huh. Miss Priss at the press. I give her the once-over. She's still too clean. No ink under *her* fingernails. Wonder what she does at *The Lily*.

I scratch my head. "Well, maybe. Problem is I've been trying to join my brother on the Erie for years. Getting real antsy about it. Cooper—my brother—he's stopping back here this summer, and I'm ready to take off with him."

"That would also be an education," Miz Bloomer says. All the women laugh, but not meanly. "Well, summer's a few months away. You can learn a lot at *The Lily* in a few months."

I shrug, wary of a trap. "Well, maybe I'll stop by. Nothin' else to do except read Miz Harrington's books. And I've read them all a few times anyway."

"I'm glad you enjoy reading, Tess. Learn as much as you can, any way you can," Miz Stanton says. "I wanted to learn more, but they wouldn't let me." She shakes her head like the memory hurts and walks off to stare at some pots and pans.

"So it's settled. You'll come to *The Lily*." Miz Bloomer looks pleased.

"Yeah, I'll come around." I feel Lucy's cat-green eyes scratch holes into my forehead.

"Wonderful! I'll look for you on Monday."

"Monday!"

Miz Bloomer smiles, waves, and the women spread out to shop.

"Hey! Want me to stick close and get you all back home?"

"No thanks, Tess, we'll be fine. Now I'll see you Monday morning. I'm serious. You have the makings of a tough reporter."

I leave the store grinning.

CHAPTER THREE

I don't make it to *The Lily*. I like Miz Bloomer and her paper but am not keen on an indoor job and having to show up every day, which Miz Bloomer would expect. I get paid for running around outside after Miz Stanton's kids and that's fun! When I tell her, she chews me out, saying I should never pass up an opportunity to learn something new.

One day, Miz Stanton asks me to stay over for a few nights, because her cousin Elizabeth Miller is visiting from Peterboro, and she needs extra help with the boys. Miz Stanton has a new baby, but that wailer ain't my trouble. I stick to the three roughnecks who already know the ropes. They dress themselves, feed themselves and traipse to the outhouse all on their own. My job is strictly entertainment.

I get a kick out of those boys' monkeyshines, but it's stern Abner Manning who gives us a roaring laugh that first evening when he comes home and finds Miz Stanton standing in his foyer in bloomers. She comes home in stitches, saying he demanded to know why she was "prancing about his respectable home like a crossbred she-male." Miz Stanton hustles me into her extra room across the side yard from Manning's library. For ten minutes, we listen to the crank rant at his poor wife and call Miz Stanton a hussy and half a dozen other silly names. He carries on like she'd paraded around his castle wearing nothin' at all!

It's funny stuff, but Miz Stanton finally blows her stack. "Why is he blaming Miranda?" she fumes. "That poor woman is strangling in a corset and long dress with crinoline underskirts and heaven knows how many petticoats." Through the window, we watch Miz Manning escape the library, panting.

"Well, she's either angry or suffering from the constricting grasp of redoubtable stays that pin her in a perpetually perpendicular position!" Miz Stanton spits the words like bullets. I double over laughing.

"Abner Manning is far behind the times," Miz Stanton pouts. "Women's pantaloons are no longer a novelty. Amelia publishes patterns for wide trousers and short skirts in nearly every edition of *The Lily*."

Miz Stanton helps her friend package pattern orders by the hundreds from women all over New York and even around the country. Other newspapers, reporting on the *Lily*'s campaign for comfortable female clothing, have nicknamed the new outfits "bloomers" after our own Amelia. She's famous!

I like bloomers and think Miz Stanton's puffy pants fit her personality—bold and boastful. Her waistline is loose and comfortable. Her skirt reaches just below her knees, instead of dragging across the floor scraping up dust, dirt, sticks, turds and gobs of spit. Miz Stanton is fashion free and like me not the least embarrassed by it, although her boys are horrified.

"Don't pick me up at school wearing that, Mother, please!" Neal begs.

Considering the messy scene this evening, I'm surprised when Miz Manning and Lucy keep Miz Stanton's invitation and knock on her front door after supper. I let them in just as cousin Elizabeth climbs the staircase carrying a candle in one hand and cradling the new baby to her shoulder with the other.

Miz Manning frowns. "Women in men's—" She can't get the word out.

"Trousers, Miranda. Say it. Trousers. Your tongue won't catch fire." Miz Stanton laughs.

"It's against scripture."

"That's Abner talking! But I am sorry you took the brunt of his wrath after I left."

"You heard?" Miz Manning's face falls.

"It's not important. What is important is how easily my cousin climbs the stairs carrying the baby. She doesn't need a third hand to hold up a heavy gown! She hops about like a spring bird."

"Try it on," cousin Elizabeth begs, when she comes back downstairs. It takes a lot of prodding, but we can see Miz Manning wants to, and she finally makes her way to the Stanton bedroom and starts peeling off layers. I know Lucy doesn't want me here, but the boys are in bed and Miz Stanton doesn't say scat, so I make myself comfortable on the floor near the long mirror.

"All right, dear." Miz Stanton giggles. "You can begin by unbuttoning that bodice." Miz Manning takes a breath, relaxes and her slim fingers tackle the buttons. "Now, what do we have underneath? Oh, a dainty camisole trimmed in lace. Remove it at once!" Everyone laughs.

"Which brings us to—*the corset*. Here, let me loosen those stays." Miz Stanton attacks the strings of Miz Manning's binding like she's rescuing a suffocating child. "Let's get you breathing."

"There must be other uses for whalebone," cousin Elizabeth ponders.

Even I breathe easier when the strings are sprung.

"Oooooh." Miz Manning places her hands over her lower back.

"That's just your kidneys moving back where God intended them." Miz Stanton smiles sympathetically. "This hourglass figure may be attractive from a man's viewpoint, but think what it does to your insides. Squashes them together. It's painful. I know. I've worn these devil's devices."

"Don't swear," Miz Manning complains goodnaturedly after her second deep breath.

"It's just another way men control women. Keep them on the brink of a dead faint then call them *delicate*. It's a trap!"

Miz Manning steps out of her wool skirt, but she's far from undressed. She drops a starched, white muslin petticoat then two flannel ones then the crinoline stiffened with horsehair that makes the whole affair balloon out in what women call high fashion. Finally, Miz Manning stands wearing only a pair of long drawers edged with lace.

Cousin Elizabeth holds Miz Manning's elbow as she steps into the new pantaloons, hops on one foot and giggles like a little girl planning something naughty.

"No, no, don't pull those ties to tightly," Miz Stanton warns. "They're only meant to hold up your bloomers, not hogtie your intestines." Cousin Elizabeth drops the short dress over Miz Manning's head, and it falls like a sack to just below her knees.

"Here, turn toward the mirror."

"Oh, I look *terrible*."

"You're very handsome! But the important thing is—how do you *feel*?"

Miz Manning looks over her shoulder at her backside. "I don't know..."

Cousin Elizabeth drops a book at Miz Manning's feet. "Pick that up."

She stoops stiff-backed, then relaxes when she realizes she can bend at the waist. "Oh, that is nice." She smiles at Lucy, who looks like she could use a little loosening up herself.

"You look beautiful, Mother. Your shoulders are relaxed and your face isn't pinched."

"Tomorrow we'll call the seamstress to measure you for your own outfit," Miz Stanton declares.

"Oh, no, Lizzie. Abner would never..."

"...wear a steel corset?"

"I could never justify...."

"...breathing with ease?"

"I could never explain..."

"...fainting less than twice a day?"

"I don't faint that often!"

"Yes, you do, Mother. You fainted yesterday before dinner."

"You fainted at my Christmas party," Miz Stanton reminds her. "And it wasn't the holiday excitement. You didn't faint yesterday because you're a fragile female. You fainted because your lungs were crushed!"

"Well..." Miz Manning turns back and forth, inspecting herself in the long mirror. "I could never justify the expense."

"Good gracious!" Miz Stanton grips her head with both hands. "How many dresses do you buy each season?"

"Not that many."

"How many?"

"Five or six. Day dresses. That doesn't include gowns."

"Does Abner question the expense?"

Miz Manning hesitates but admits, "Never."

"Have you ordered your summer wardrobe yet?"

"A few pieces." Miz Manning smiles at Lucy smiling at her in the mirror. She really is a pretty lady.

"Wonderful! Have your seamstress make you one or two of these outfits."

"Oh, my goodness! I could never wear this in public."

"Do it, Mother!"

"Try just one, Miranda," cousin Elizabeth begs. "Wear it around the house. You'll love it. It'll be all you wear. But if I'm wrong, and if you don't like it, order a closet full of those Iron Maidens."

I shiver. The Iron Maiden. I'd read in one of Miz Harrington's books about that torture box used during the Spanish Inquisition. Now I'm positive Lucy wears a corset. She picks at her sides and her face is always pinched. And I always thought she was just moody.

"Can't you just give up the corset and wear the dresses you have?" I ask.

"Oh, if only it were that easy." Miz Manning smiles at me. "But none of them would fit. The seamstress sewed them to fit when I'm corseted."

She drops the book on the floor again and bends swiftly to retrieve it. Her face isn't fiery red when she stands up.

"Think how easy gardening will be," Miz Stanton says.

"Women deserve to be comfortable," cousin Elizabeth adds.

I find out a week later that Miz Manning never ordered a bloomer outfit. Miz Stanton tells me that when grouchy Abner stood on his porch smoking one evening and saw her parading outside in pantaloons, herding her boys in for bedtime, he nearly swallowed his cigar.

"I can not believe Henry Stanton allows his wife to shame him in such manner," she heard him grumble to Miz Manning on his way back inside. Miz Stanton roars like a muleskinner when she tells me.

CHAPTER FOUR

"Tess Riley is absolutely the scourge of my existence."

I'm taking out Miz Stanton's trash when Priss' snarl licks my ear.

"She's a hard girl to keep up with," Miz Manning says. They're inside their screened porch, lolling away the afternoon.

"She talks like a ruffian and dresses like a beggar, but her brain is lightning fast." Is that a compliment? I quietly set the heavy lid back on the trash can and tiptoe across the side yard, settling myself in the grass below the porch. Now if those Stanton brats will just stay inside, I'll learn what little Lucy really thinks of me.

I've been setting type at *The Lily* for two weeks now—ever since Miz Stanton grabbed my ear and dragged me over there—and just stopped on Washington Street to mind the boys for an hour while she straightens up the house. Her husband is coming home from Albany. Henry Stanton is an abolitionist like Lucy's old man, but has political goals that take him out of town regularly.

I wonder what old Henry will say about the remodeling Miz Stanton did while he was gone. Sick of dealing with the kids by herself, she called in a carpenter to knock out a section of wall and put in a new window. She does that often. Says it brightens up her life.

"She certainly learned how to set type quickly." Miz Manning takes a sip of something. "Amelia says she's very intelligent."

"You'd never know by looking at her."

"Don't be unkind. Tess works hard. She spends long hours in that press room."

"She smells like dirt."

"She has pretty eyes. Large and dark."

"She's as big as a man! I would never want broad shoulders like that. She can hardly move around the printing press. Stands like she's in a rum-hole, one arm on the doorjamb, hip cocked."

"You should never criticize someone's appearance, Lucy."

"Well, then I suppose you don't want me to say she grins like a monkey when Mrs. Bloomer hands her a pay envelope."

Lucy Manning. The Mouth. For someone who's supposed to "show me the ropes," she's doing a lousy job. She ignores me, refuses to answer my questions. When I go to Miz Bloomer for help, the bootlicker acts like I tattled.

"What she does with her money is a mystery to me. She certainly doesn't spend it on clothes. The first week she wore those disgusting hand-hacked trouser-skirts they raved about at the mercantile. Wiped her inky hands on them and they got dirtier and dirtier."

"Tess probably can't afford to spend her earnings on pretty clothes."

"Pretty and Tess do not go together. And can you believe Mrs. Bloomer suggested she just wear men's pants! They walked over to the church basement, and I thought I'd faint when they came back with five pairs of men's trousers. Now Tess wears them every day. Struts around like the President!"

"Consider them an improvement, dear."

"She's like some Dickens street scamp. Hair's short as a man's and she wears that stupid newsboy's cap—backwards—on her nearly bald head. Who's she supposed to be? Oliver Twist?"

"I think you spend too much time thinking about Tess. Of course, if your father catches on to what we're doing at *The Lily*, you'll be spared that aggravation. I'm afraid it's only a matter of time before he does."

There's a short silence. I paw the grass for four leaf clovers.

"And if he finds out about your other enterprise, Lucy, there will be hell to pay."

"Mother, I do believe that's the first time I've ever heard you say *hell*." She whispers "*hell*" like her tongue might melt. "But Father will never find out. My money's well hidden. He never comes to my room. How would he catch me?"

They're silent for a while. Her *other* enterprise? What's Lucy up to besides moping around *The Lily*? And she hides money, too? Definitely the only thing we have in common.

"Can't you be friends with Tess?"

"Oh, Mother, she's just awful! She leaves *The Lily* with ink smudged all over her face and neck. Never looks in a mirror!" I pull out handfuls of grass and throw them at my feet. Dang, let it go, girl.

"Smudges and all, Amelia thinks the world of Tess."

"Well, I guess the amount of ink on her face doesn't hurt profits."

I hear Kit Stanton calling me from inside the house.

"If she just wouldn't spit! It's revolting. Is she chewing tobacco? Another disgusting habit she picked up on that towpath?"

"Oh, Lucy, you haven't actually seen tobacco in her mouth?"

"UGH! If I saw a thick, gooey wad of gunk in her cheek…If Mrs. Bloomer saw it dripping on the press…"

I have to stop myself from jumping onto the porch and punching her pointy little chin. I just like spitting. It's just spit, for cripes sake.

"Well, maybe she wouldn't care. According to Mrs. Bloomer, Tess Riley can do no wrong," Lucy whines. "Tess is just *sooooo wonderful.*"

Can't take the competition, huh? It's true, Miz Bloomer took to me like a pig to slop. She's thrilled because I'm even smarter and quicker than she thought I was, and she started teaching me to work the printing press after just one week. I might talk loose, but thanks to all Miz Harrington's books I can spell like a champ. And setting type only makes me smarter. I catch mistakes in handwritten stories, and Lucy's ma says there are very few errors on the proof sheets. Miz Bloomer says there's been "a marked improvement in the general quality of the newspaper," since I've been setting type. In just two weeks! When she heard that, Lucy stalked home grumbling.

"Well, no one gives me credit for helping Tess with her spelling. The first day she was there, Mrs. Bloomer came right over to me. '*Lucy, you're not doing anything. Copy these words from the dictionary for Tess to practice later, would you, please?*'"

Now I wish I hadn't played along. I knew how to spell those words years ago. I was just being agreeable for Miz Bloomer's sake.

"And today, '*Lucy, sweep the floor around the printing press, so Tess doesn't get tangled up in paper scraps.*' Really, Mother, I'm not the maid."

"Well, you can always stay home and…" Miz Manning's voice trails off.

And what? Stay home and *what?*

After a pause, Lucy says, "I know. I should. But I hate the tight, anxious feeling I get when Tess is at *The Lily* and I'm not."

Considering the tight rein old Manning keeps on his women, I wonder how they can steal away to *The Lily* every afternoon. What lies are they telling him?

Miz Stanton told me Lucy graduated from Galworth's School for Girls last spring. And I heard Miz Manning complain to Miz Stanton that when Lucy turned seventeen her pa groused she was well on her way to spinsterhood. The day after her graduation party (no, I wasn't invited), he fired a servant and insisted Lucy pitch in with the housework.

"A training exercise, I suppose, for her approaching career as nursemaid to Jeremy or Freeman's children" Miz Stanton told me, grim-faced. "He also makes her take classes in flower arranging, tatting and he just

bought a pianoforte. God help the man." She scowled. "He's plotting, bringing home what he calls '*fine young men*,' fully expecting one to take Lucy
off his hands." Yeah, I saw them, too. Stiff buttoned gangly gawky guys
with slicked-down hair following Manning home for dinner.

Cripes, if Lucy wasn't mean as a mosquito, I'd feel sorry for her. It
must have been hard watching her brother hustle off to Yale last September.
Miz Stanton said she had no idea how Manning got Jeremy accepted into
the university. Even with tutoring—on his wife's money—the boy's
entrance exams had been "unimpressive." No wonder Lucy's miserable.
She still has her heart set on going to college and being a lawyer and has no
way to get there.

Well, Lucy and her ma got jobs at *The Lily* somehow and for some
reason the old coot hasn't gone wrathy as a ghoul. Strange, because *The
Lily* isn't his kind of newspaper.

Miz Bloomer started publishing it early last year as a temperance
paper. She'd formed the Ladies Temperance Society in Seneca Falls a few
months earlier, because she felt the men weren't giving the women enough
credit for their hard work in the movement.

But when the Tennessee Legislature declared women couldn't own
property because they didn't have souls, Miz Bloomer had a conniption fit.
In the next issue of *The Lily*, she wrote it was "high time that women...open
their eyes and look where they stand. It is quite time that their rights should
be discussed, and that woman herself should enter the contest." From then
on Miz Bloomer was a tough-talking supporter of the women's movement,
adding "Devoted to the Interests of Women" to *The Lily* nameplate.

I can tell Lucy loves the newspaper. She's proud when Miz Bloomer
asks her for a word to improve a sentence. She likes proofreading and is
jealous of the two stringers who cover town and village meetings.

Some days—I think the days I get on her nerves just by being good at
my job—she hides out in the women's center Miz Bloomer set up next door
that has newspapers from all over the country. I went in there once or twice,
but got fed up with old ladies blabbing every horrible-husband story you
can think of. Some have righteous complaints: their husbands are mean,
stingy, rough. But I can't stand petty crabbing. You'd think grown men and
women could work out problems like who to invite for Christmas dinner or
what to name the cat.

Maybe it gets to Lucy, too, because sometimes she misses a day or
two at *The Lily* and when she comes back she's in an even worse mood and
her fingers are red and sore. It looks like she even has calluses on those
dainty tips, but that can't be. Unless playing the pianoforte is blistering
work.

CHAPTER FIVE

Lucy flips the broom with a loud clang behind the printing press, and she's dang lucky I don't drop the type tray. I look up, mad as a March hare, and jerk my hand across my nose.

"Land sakes, Tess, you just turned your face black as a boot!" She does her little parade spin and stomps out of the press room. I set the tray down and follow. The girl's asking for trouble.

"I want to write a story, Mrs. Bloomer," she whines when Amelia comes toward us with a sheaf of handwritten articles.

"About what, Lucy?" She gives me a wondering look. I shrug.

"About anything!" Lucy leans against the newsroom counter, arms across her chest. Her frown makes her sharp, thin face look like a skull and crossbones.

"Do I detect boredom, Lucy?"

"Yes! Absolute complete and total boredom. I've read all the newspapers and magazines. I've listened to everyone next door gripe about their husbands. I want to get out of this office, but I don't want to go home!"

Her ma, sitting at a long table shuffling proof sheets, taps her chin with her pencil and crinkles her forehead with worry.

"I received A's in composition," Lucy mumbles lamely, then scowls when she sees me braced against the doorjamb.

"Oh, I know you're smart, dear...It's just that..."

"Your father would not approve, Lucy," Miz Manning says. "He'll see your name."

I stretch and yawn in the doorway. "You could make up a fake one."

"Mind your own business!" Whoa, there girly. You're playing with fire. "If I write for *The Lily* I want *my* name on it! Nobody's going to cheat me out of the credit. Women get cheated out of everything. Mother, I won't let him hold me back. Mrs. Bloomer, please, is there something, anything, I can write about?"

"Well, tonight's town meeting is already covered...but...the circus is coming to town."

I bust out laughing. Lucy's face flames red. If she had a club I'd be defending my life. I mumble "kid stuff" under my breath.

"I don't care! I'll do it! I'll write about the circus!" She turns her back on me. "I'll follow the parade. I'll talk to the elephant driver."

"Really, Amelia, I don't think this is appropriate for Lucy," her ma complains. "Abner won't..."

"Don't tell him, Mother! Oh, tell him! I don't care what he says." The Priss is bold, but her ma's nervous.

"Circus hands are rough, vulgar...you're so young."

"Mother! I'm seventeen years old! Some of my former classmates have babies!"

"I'll take her."

Lucy spins around like I've snagged her with a whip.

"I'll take her down to the circus grounds."

"I don't need anyone to *take* me. You're not even as old as me."

"I can handle circus toughs."

"I bet you can—being a rowdy yourself."

"Lucy! Apologize to Tess." Miz Manning throws me a sympathetic look.

The Priss crosses her arms and pouts. If her ma and Miz Bloomer weren't here, I'd fix her flint.

"It's a good idea," Miz Bloomer says. "There's safety in numbers, Miranda. And truthfully, neither of them are children."

"I'll keep an eye on her, Miz Manning." I smile politely.

Lucy's lips part as she grits her teeth.

"You want out of here, don't you?" I smile smugly.

A brief pause. "All right, you can come."

"Whoooeeee, thanks." I head back to the pressroom.

"Yes, please resume smearing ink on your face."

I toss a dangerous look over my shoulder. Let's see how bold she is when her ma's not around.

CHAPTER SIX

"Mama's gonna be mad, Tessie, I go off without her."

"Shut up, whiner! This is a treat!" I pull Beany down the front steps and head up Fall Street.

"Where we going?"

"To the circus." It's kid stuff, so I'm bringing a kid.

"They won't let me in!"

I talked about the circus for two days, but never said nothin' about Beany going. I wanted it to be a surprise.

"Yeah, they will. Two press passes will get us on the grounds. One for me and one for you."

"Mama says I can't go anywhere without her."

"Well, I'm saying you can. This is special. You like to draw, right?"

"Yeah."

"Well, at the circus there's animals you never saw before except in Miz Harrington's travel books. Wild animals."

"Wild!"

I snort and nudge Beany toward the center of town where the parade will start. "You got your pad and charcoal Miz Harrington gave you for your birthday?"

"Mama gonna kill me if I lose it. Mama gonna kill me for coming to town with you, anyway."

"Shut up with that 'Mama gonna kill me' crap. Live a little, you little loony. You're always cooped up in that house. You got no friends."

"And who'd be friends with me? Nobody knows me."

"That's what I mean."

"You know me and you're not my friend."

I stop dead, glare at her, then stalk up the street. She follows like I know she will.

"Fix your hair, we're gonna meet the Queen of Seneca Falls."

"What?" Beany's hands jump to her curls.

I laugh. "Just kidding. I mean Miss Priss." We weave through a crowd moving toward the parade's starting point.

"She's coming?" Beany looks down at her thin, dull dress.

"Yeah, I'm her guard dog. Told her ma I'll protect her from the big bad circus clowns."

Lucy waits in front of the general store. "You're late."

"This is Beany." I look up the street for signs of action.

"Yes, I know Beany." Lucy smiles. "Doesn't Miss Harrington call you Willow?" Beany nods and hides behind me. Some little kids in fancy suits point at Beany and giggle.

"Scram, river rats!" I swipe at them, and their snooty mothers yank them away.

"I wanna go home, Tessie."

"Nope. Your gonna see this parade, then you're going to the circus grounds to draw the animals. You, me and Miss...uh, Lucy, here...are gonna breathe this circus air for two days."

"Two days! Never mind, I'll be dead tonight, Mama hears I been on Fall Street."

Lucy's face twitches with an awkward smile.

"Don't pay attention to her fussing. Got your notebook?"

"Of course I do." Lucy's shoulders jerk irritably.

"Well, get it out. I hear music!"

"Don't boss me!"

We turn toward a blaring racket marching toward us like a threat.

Beany claps her hands over her ears. "That ain't pretty."

I point out the animals ambling down Fall Street, pretending I'm leading a safari like I read about in travel books. First come the elephants, big and round, their long, thick noses hanging on to the tiny tails of the beasts in front of them. Some guy dressed in stripes with flaming cheeks and a red nose he must have slammed in a door comes behind them swinging a broom.

Cages with thick bars roll by carrying cats fifty times bigger then Ma's striped tabby, and when they roar a shiver runs up my back that makes me feel I'm sliding across an icy pond.

Lucy scribbles fast. Every now and then I point and shout out something she missed, and she writes that down, too, but gets madder and madder about me bossing her. A tall, skinny guy beating a big, round drum passes us. BOOM! BOOM! BOOM! Beany likes that better than the blaring horns.

A weird creature with a humpy back wobbles past and some fool's riding it! Swaying side to side like he's about to fall off. Fancy gals wrapped in strips of cloth twirl by and bow and leap and bow and leap, like they can't make up their minds if they want to be up or down. They need better clothes—looks like bandages falling off.

When Beany shrieks, Lucy and I laugh.

"That is not from this world." Beany's head tips back and her mouth hangs open. The creature rides in a wagon twice as tall as the cat cages, but the wagon top is cut open and its tiny head—wagging on a long, thin neck—peers into the second story windows of the buildings on Fall Street. It has little knobby horns, but kind of a pretty face for a thing so misshapen. Behind the bars I see a round spotty body and long, skinny legs.

"What's that, Tessie?"

"I dunno. Saw it in a book but forgot the name."

"It's a giraffe," Lucy says smugly. "From Africa."

Beany stares at Lucy like she's the smartest gal in Seneca Falls, which in Beany's case means the whole world.

"Most of these animals come from Africa. The lions and elephants. The camels are from northern Africa. Maybe Egypt."

"Come on," I say, budging into the schoolmarm lesson. "Parade's almost over. Let's get down to the fairgrounds." I push Beany ahead of me and Lucy has to run to catch us.

"You sure scribble a lot." At the fairgrounds I peek at Lucy's pencil scratching, but the big bug newspaper reporter slams her notebook shut. "I ain't stealing nothin'." Lucy turns her back. "Go on flip your snooty nose in the air."

Beany sits on a stack of logs a few yards from the giraffe. She can't keep her eyes off it. One of the animal keepers puts a hay bale in a basket atop a tall pole and the giraffe reaches for its lunch. Its lower jaw slides from side to side like a lazy saw. Beany watches the beast bug-eyed and rubs her charcoal pencil across her pad. A small smile slides along her lips.

"Why don't you ask that handler about that giraffe?"

"Don't boss me! I know my job. Besides, I like the cats better."

"They stink."

"They don't *stink*. They have their own natural odor—same as you."

My face gets hot. "Are you saying…?"

"Oh, for land sakes don't get huffy!"

"Why are you in a pucker?"

"I'm not *in a pucker*! I'm trying to work. It's my job to write stories. How I do it is none of your business."

"Did Miz Bloomer tell you what to write about?"

"*Nooo*." Lucy says the word carefully, trying to be patient with me, a big, dumb oaf. "Mind your own business."

"Mind yours, pucker puss."

Lucy sucks in so much air she starts hacking like a sick mule—BOK! BOK! BOK! She finally catches her breath and stumbles off mumbling something about a lion tamer. Good riddance.

I'm dozing, Beany's drawing a few feet away, when a grizzled carnie growls, "Hey, you—blackie. Get off those logs!" I jump up, wide awake. The guy's big, too big to take, so I haul Beany off to another cage.

"Where's Lucy? Aren't you supposed to watch her?"

"I hope she ends up lion lunch." I flop down in front of a large ape that stares back at me with sad, wet eyes. Beany settles down, turns to a clean page and draws the ape's head. Wouldn't Priss have a conniption fit if I wrote a newspaper story? That was Miz Bloomer's original plan, but I got hooked on printing. If I did write a story, I know it'd be better than Lucy's.

Another hour and it's time to head home. "Let's go, Bean."

"I'm not done." She's drawn the black ape at least six times. It looks like it's walking across the page.

"Finish tomorrow. We'll be back."

"He'll change, won't be the same animal."

I tempt her with popcorn and candy apples, but the squirt won't lift her head.

"Look, Bean, I really hate forcing you, seeing as how you're actually having a good time for once in your life, but I'm tuckered out."

"You ain't done nothin' but sit all day."

"Well, aren't you the smarty pants? Hey! Is that your mama calling?" That gets her attention.

Beany snatches up her pad and charcoal and follows me across the circus grounds. We're almost to the road when I remember. "Shoot! Miss Priss."

Where the heck is she? We walk from tent to tent, cage to cage, until we hear a squeaky laugh and follow it to the monkeys.

"Land sakes!" Some skinny, hairy thing is crawling across Lucy's shoulders. She's balancing the spidery beast on her arm, talking to the monkey keeper, and trying to write. I can't believe prim Priss is pals with a primate!

"Come on, Luce. We're leaving." I scuff the dirt impatiently with my toe. She gabs with the monkey man. A minute goes by, then another. "Hey! Beany and me are heading back."

"Go! It's not like I don't know my way home," she snaps. The little monkey wraps its arms around her head and grins, flashing sharp teeth. I can't tell which one is uglier.

I mumble something foul and spit in the dirt. "I'm supposed to be watching you."

Lucy's face turns tomato red. "Don't be ridiculous! Go home!" Turning her back, she coos to the monkey and makes kissing noises.

Okay, let someone grab her. Beany and I take off, but when I glance back, Lucy's hopping after us, her face bright as Miz Stanton's sunny yellow floors. While we wait for her to catch up, I reach for Beany's pictures. She opens her pad shyly.

"WOW! Those are some clowns! I thought you were stuck on that giraffe. Look, Luce." The real-life parade clown I remember was dumpy and clumsy. Beany's drawing keeps his odd shape, but gives him grace and humor.

"My name is Lucy. Not Luce. Lucy." In the same breath she adds, "I like that, Beany—and, since we're on the subject of proper names—should I call you Willow? Willow is very pretty. And it suits you more."

Beany shifts her sketches from hand to hand. "Um, I like Willow. Never liked Beany."

"Everybody calls her Beany." I turn to go.

"Miz Harrington calls me Willow."

"That's because she feels sorry for you," I snap.

"Why does she feel sorry?" Beany's chocolate eyes look hurt.

"Because you're colored, ninny. And because your ma's a slave. Let's go."

"Mama's not a slave! She's free!"

"She's a runaway."

"No she's ain't!"

"Tess, leave her alone!"

"Shut up!" I elbow Lucy then turn toward Beany. "She got papers?"

Beany looks worried. "What kind?"

"Saying her owner let her go."

"I dunno."

"Well, she doesn't, because she's a runaway."

"Tess!"

"Scram!" I show Lucy my back and turn Beany toward home. "You might be free because you were born up north…maybe." We're two miles from town, it's late afternoon and I'm tuckered out, even if I did doze in the hay most of the day. And I'm real sick of Miss Priss, who just won't shut pan.

She bustles up alongside me. "What do you mean *might*? Of course she's free."

"There's no proof where Beany was born. No proof how old she really is."

"I'm thirteen!" Beany's ready to bawl.

"There's nothin' written down."

"Mama says I was born on a canal boat and she's counted up thirteen of my years."

"Yeah, well, your mama can say anything she wants. It's what the slave catchers say that counts."

Tears pool in Beany's big eyes. "Don't talk about slave catchers, Tessie, they scare me."

Lucy takes Beany's arm and throws me a mean look. "Come on, Willow. Let's watch those men raise the big tent." She turns the kid toward some roughnecks standing around a huge piece of canvas lying on the ground.

"Hey, we gotta get back!"

Beany throws one hurt look over her shoulder and lets Lucy lead her away. She opens her pad and pulls the charcoal around on the paper. When I stalk up Lucy moves away, forcing me to follow.

"Why are you tormenting her about slave catchers?" Her green eyes flicker like shadows on a murky pond. "That's cruel."

"That's life."

"It scares her and there's no point to it."

"You heard Miz Bloomer. They're coming this way."

"Slave catchers? I don't believe it."

"My brother ran into a couple in Hammondsport last month."

Lucy's red brows pull together. I'd seen that face at *The Lily*.

"Don't take it so hard. They're not after you."

Lucy taps her notebook with her pencil. "But Willow and her mother..."

"Well, it's August's fault. I don't know why she didn't keep going when she got this far north. Most runaways keep hoofing 'til they cross the big lake to Canada. That's what folks say, anyway."

"Are those slave catchers your brother met...does he know if they're coming through Seneca Falls?" There's fear in her voice.

"Didn't say. But if not them then others some day. The ones Coop met are just loafing. Don't seem to be in a hurry. Spend most of their time in the groggery boozing and playing cards. Chances are good they'll get thrown in jail for some kind of troublemaking."

Lucy chews her pencil. "They might not even get here. Maybe they'll go west instead of north." She seems all-fired concerned for somebody who barely knows two colored folks.

Lucy walks back to Beany sitting cross-legged on the ground, caught up in her drawing. When the Bean looks up shyly, Lucy drops down on the ground beside her, shoulder to shoulder, and smiles.

CHAPTER SEVEN

I'm sold on this newspaper business. I don't even mind being cooped up inside setting type and running the press. It's hard work, but I'm good at it and Miz Bloomer raves about me. It used to scrape the skin off Miss Priss, but she doesn't care anymore because Miz Bloomer raves about her, too. She was so tickled with Lucy's circus stories she gives her one assignment a day now, enough to make the prickly puss chuck her pickle nose. I still tag along, but we've formed a truce: I don't call her pucker puss, and she doesn't tell me to shut pan. And I'm glad she works for *The Lily*. I'm not going soft. I just like her stories. They aren't dry sermons about what happened when. She always gets somebody to say something funny, touching, silly or damning.

People tell Lucy the darndest things. She has some magic that makes her victims spill their guts. She smiles a lot, listens hard and breaks down the barriers. She's so good, she's squeezed out one of the regular stringers and spends long hours at the newspaper office. So I guess it's no surprise her old man's gone savage as a meat ax.

Yeah, old Abner gave her misery from the very first circus story. Lucy said her little brother showed him the paper with her name below the headline soon as he came home. I would have wrung the guttersnipe's neck. I was helping out at the Stantons and heard Manning charging around like a mad bull, yelling that no daughter of his was gonna be a newspaper reporter. And for *The Lily* no less! Full of female bunkum. He ordered her to stop.

When Lucy escaped to the front porch, I went outside and saw her flopped down on the step, head buried in her arms, like she'd been flogged. I sidled across the lawn.

"Hey, Luce." She looked up quickly, eyes red as her hair, then dropped her head again. It was the day after our first assignment, and we weren't exactly chums. I expected her to yell "SCAT!" but she just sobbed into her knees, heartbroken.

I dug a hole in the dirt with my toe and watched her bawl, then touched her shoulder. "Hey, don't let him stop you." She jerked her head up. "Yeah, keep at it, girl, you're good at it." I left her to her tears and walked home.

Lucy's come to work every day since, but she's taking a beating. I'm at the Stanton house every evening when the printing's done and can hear her old man blustering like a buffoon about her prancing around with a barefoot tomboy, hanging around women in pants. Yesterday, he dragged her and her ma into that dark library and scared the dickens out of them. I snuck into the guest room and tried to listen, but this time there wasn't any shouting. And today, Miz Manning walks into the *Lily* newsroom and busts out crying, and Miz Bloomer has to take her into her office and calm her down. I know Abner Manning's making wicked threats.

Lucy's scared, but mad. "I love my mother, Tess, but I'm not going to end up like her."

I settle on a stool in the printing room. Lucy huddles near the wall, arms crossed over her middle like her belly aches.

"My mother is an intelligent woman, even though she has no education. Unfortunately, she also has no occupation, which means if something happens to my father, or…" she stops and tears slide down her cheeks…"or if…she has to leave…" she plucks at her nose with a lacy handkerchief…"she'll have no means to support herself." Lucy covers her eyes and her shoulders shake. I have a good idea what she's talking about.

"I swear, Tess, I will never allow anyone to control my life! Not my father, not any man, ever!" I see now that Lucy's a lot tougher than her fancy clothes and prissy talk led me to believe. "My mother has been ordered about her whole life. Told what she can and can't do—what she can and can't think—but it won't happen to me! I won't let it!"

She drops her arms and holds them stiffly at her sides. "I am a reporter for *The Lily* and I am not quitting!"

Each day gets worse and by the end of the week something real nasty hits and Lucy stays overnight at Miz Bloomer's house. The next day old Abner shows up at *The Lily* in a powerful pucker.

"Get my daughter!" he orders, keeping his eyes off Amelia's bloomers.

"Lucy isn't here. She's out working on a story."

I hang in the pressroom doorway, a hunk of lead in one hand. I might owe Manning something for helping August, but if he gets rough with Miz Bloomer I won't hesitate using this lead slug.

"She spent the night at your house without my permission. Only the threat of an ugly scene prevented me from breaking down your door."

Miz Bloomer watches him calmly from behind the counter. "Lucy is always welcome…"

"Not unless I permit it, and I did not. When she returns, send her right home. Do you understand?"

Miz Bloomer nods. "I understand you want her home."

I glance out the printing room window and see Lucy crossing the street, grinning after another successful interview. I slip outside, put my finger to my lips, pull her into the shop's side door and stuff her behind the type cabinet.

"Send her home!" Manning charges through the front door, growling threats about finding the constable. I make Lucy stay hidden for a full half hour.

Manning doesn't come back, but the next day I hear how his wife spent the night at Miz Bloomer's, too. While her ma sits in the newsroom, tears pouring like Niagara Falls on the proof sheets, Lucy and I sit beside the printing press, and she blurts out how her pa's threatened to divorce her ma. Says her ma'd have to leave their house, and the kids would have to stay there with old Abner, just like Miz Stanton said.

"I don't want to lose my mother. I don't know if I can do this."

"Don't know…? Whoa there! Your ma doesn't want you to quit *The Lily*. If she did, there wouldn't be this ruckus and she wouldn't be here right now instead of home patching your old man's pants." After a moment I ask, "Did she leave or did he throw her out?"

"I don't know." Lucy wrings her hands. "I'm so confused. When I left two days ago, I told him I was old enough to be on my own. I had a job and I didn't have to stay there and be bullied."

Man alive! Most gals either get married young or hang on with their folks 'til they're old, gray and dead. Lucy's ready to go it on her own!

Lucy says last night her father browbeat her mother, harping and yelling about Lucy taking refuge at Miz Bloomer's house the night before. Miz Manning finally told him she was fed up with his hounding and walked out the door, but she was sick about it. It broke her heart to leave little Freeman who cried watching her go.

I don't know what to say. My pa's a holy terror, but he doesn't give a hoot what I do.

Lucy's laugh surprises me. "The night I left, he said he wasn't fooled. He knew his wife was working at *The Lily*. Working! As if that was the most horrible, humiliating thing a wife could do to her husband. If it wasn't so awful, it would be funny. I mean if it happened to someone else and not mother and me."

"Well, I don't get how you and your ma ever took jobs here in the first place. He doesn't strike me as a man easily hornswoggled."

Lucy wipes her eyes and smiles weakly. "You're right. We fooled him. Or Mother did. But only for a while. Mother and I loved *The Lily* from the start. It's not like that horrid *Godey's Ladies Book* he buys for her, full of propaganda about a 'woman's sphere.' I read it out of curiosity and am sickened by its twisted view of the ideal feminine image."

Lucy says that, according to *Godey's*—and every other woman's magazine she's read—the ideal woman is gentle, patient, unassuming and all-enduring. She's a wife and a mother. She has no strong feelings or needs of her own. She hides her true emotions. She hides her intelligence, especially. Same for any knowledge or talents she might have.

"The ideal woman tucks everything that's best or novel or precious about her into some dark corner of her soul where her husband won't be threatened by it."

I stare at Lucy, struck dumb by her passion.

"Mrs. Bloomer's articles encourage women to be vigorous and courageous, not feeble and spineless. Women can be gentle and patient, but also dynamic and ingenious when called upon to break the bonds of male-imposed subservience."

I laugh. "Lordy, Luce, you talk like a book."

She raises that pointy little chin a notch. "I'm so proud of Mother for coming here to work. She has an outlet for her creativity and she's out-smarting Father. According to him, well-bred women with successful husbands don't work." Lucy waves her hand and bats her eyelashes.

I laugh again, glad she's having a little fun.

"Society frowns on such brassy behavior. It was an education to hear Mother convince Father that her activity at *The Lily* was trivial, a frivolous pursuit, pure entertainment."

"Yeah, and how'd she do that?" I pull out a type tray and start spelling out a story.

Lucy says that at first Miz Manning told her husband she was just doing her small part for the temperance movement by proofreading short articles on her way to market when Miz Bloomer got busy. She didn't dare tell him Amelia was paying her a salary. When Manning said *The Lily* really wasn't a temperance newspaper anymore, his wife pulled a copy from under a stack of *Godey's* and pointed out each article that mentioned it.

She read aloud stories about wives and children being beaten by drunken husbands and drunken husbands gambling away their wives' inheritances. When Manning said he still didn't approve of *The Lily*, his wife pointedly threw it in the trash.

"Didn't he complain about her not running the house?" I glance out the pressroom window, expecting the big buffalo to blast in any minute.

Lucy says her ma made sure the servants kept the house clean and orderly. Old man Manning's shirts were starched and ironed without a wrinkle. Miz Manning was always home when her husband walked in the door at six o'clock. Meals were on the table promptly.

"Truthfully, he found nothing to complain about."

"Yeah, but didn't his cronies give him a hard time? He was so all-fired *embarrassed* when you went to Miz Stanton's convention."

"I heard him telling another lawyer that his wife had simply taken the temperance movement to heart. If it kept her happy…and here's the sticky part…'*if it stops her persistent nagging about Lucy*'…so much the better."

"Your ma nags him about you?"

"You know, about college."

"You still want to do that?"

"Of course!"

I won't fight her on it. She has enough problems. "So what went wrong?"

"I started writing. Mother had never written for *The Lily*. But I signed my name to a story in a newspaper he disliked. Here's where your public humiliation comes in. He turned into a madman."

I can't stop from asking, "So…do you think he'll … make her leave? *Divorce* her?"

Lucy shutters at the word, stares at me with watery eyes. "I don't know." Her voice is twisted, strained. She says her ma sent him a note saying she'd be gone for a few days to give him time to calm down. He sent a note back saying she should use the time to come to her senses. And when she does—when she returns home—to bring Lucy with her.

We hear Miz Manning throwing up and Miz Bloomer sends me to get the midwife to concoct some special tea to soothe her sick stomach. Lucy refuses an interview assignment to sit with her ma, but I can see she's conflicted—doesn't want to feel her old man conned her into not working. I end up doing the interview, just to help out. When I get back, the three of them are still huddled in Miz Bloomer's office.

"Oh, while I had my doubts, I generally accepted that men knew best." Miz Manning's voice is raspy from crying. "That there were things I couldn't do that men could do better for me." She wipes her puffy eyes. "But I won't accept that any longer."

I lean against the wall. Lucy's face is blotchy and her nose runs.

Miz Manning says they argued every day about Lucy going to college. A few years ago Lucy wanted to go to Rebecca Harrington's academy and he refused to take her out of Galworth's. He said what was good enough for his wife was good enough for his daughter.

"But I say no it isn't! I want something better for my children, especially for my daughter." Miz Manning sits up straighter in her chair. "He mocked me. When I told him Lizzie Stanton learned Greek, he laughed. '*What's the point? Are you exchanging recipes in Greek?*'"

Lucy wraps an arm around her ma's shoulder. "He talked to Mother's cousin in Buffalo about taking me on as nanny to his children. I refused to go. I sent him a note saying there's more to life than tending children and husband, and I intend to get a lot more."

I know that went over like peas in a punchbowl.

Miz Manning sips her healing tea. "I told him about Elizabeth Blackwell attending the Geneva medical school. I admitted she was having trouble being accepted by the male students. They treat her poorly."

She says Manning scoffed and demanded to know if that was what she wanted for her daughter. Said she was dull-witted if she thought the same thing wouldn't happen in law school.

"Lucy's a strong girl." Miz Bloomer stands tall, sturdy as a warrior. "She'll survive. In fact, she'll thrive!"

Miz Manning shakes her head. "He said he's not paying for some lunatic social experiment. That's when I lost my temper. I asked him why not? Why not be counted among those who change society. We should *make* them accept her. We should *insist* upon it!"

"A young woman must be allowed to grow, mentally as well as physically." Miz Bloomer looks from Lucy to me. "She must be respected as an individual. Not tolerated as someone's daughter or mother or wife."

The misery lasts two long weeks and feeds town gossip at every fencepost. But today, out of the blue, Abner Manning shows up and in a tight voice asks to speak to his wife in private. I've had my fill of the tyrant and stand guard in the pressroom doorway, tossing my hunk of lead from hand to hand. Miz Bloomer and Lucy insist on sticking around, too, so Manning has an audience, while he cuts a deal with his wife. When it's over, I can't believe the hogwash.

After all the shouting, stomping, puking, tea and tears, all Manning demands is that his wife and daughter stay trussed up in their corsets and long skirts—they have to swear off bloomers—keep their long hair—he eyes my stubbly head—and be home by six o'clock. What a bag o' bunkum. I almost laugh out loud, but don't want to mock Lucy or hurt her ma's feelings.

But after he leaves I say, "Don't be hornswaggled, ma'am. It's a trick."

"No, Tess, he's serious." I'm surprised Miz Manning can see me through her red, swollen eyes.

"Those are little kid rules." Cripes, nobody's told me when to come in at night since I was twelve years old."

"It may sound childish, but I'm claiming victory." Her puffy face beams like a full moon.

"It appears Father can't handle the scandal of tossing his wife and daughter out on the street." Lucy has her arm around her ma. "And he doesn't want to be left alone with Freeman."

"He couldn't get what he wanted with brawn and bluster," Miz Bloomer says, smiling wickedly. "So he's saving face."

"Yes, he is worried about his reputation. Maybe even his law practice. Better to quiet the whole thing down." Miz Manning lays her head on Lucy's shoulder. They're both tiny.

They think they've called his bluff and won. I think it's a lot of humbug, and it turns out I'm partly right. Lucy comes to work the next day angry, yet victorious. The thing on her pa's mind now is money.

"He wanted to know what that '*saucy Bloomer woman*' is paying me. I said practically nothing—a quarter a story."

"You lied to him, just like that?" The girl learns fast. Truth is Lucy's earning what the stringer earned, decent money.

"He scoffed, said it was a pittance, but in the next breath demanded my salary. When I told him I'm saving that money for college, he burst out laughing. '*Keep your little job and your little salary*,' he said. '*Save your quarters for Oberlin.*'"

She tries to hide the quiver in her voice by rustling papers. "He thinks I'm a joke, but I don't care."

"Good. You shouldn't care. Telling him you're saving quarters for college gets him off your back. He thinks you can't do it. You're not a threat."

"But I will do it, Tess!"

"I know you will." Personally, I think she can spend her money on better things. I've been thinking about her and me taking off on the canal, getting newspaper jobs somewhere out west.

"The important thing is I stood up to him. I don't care that I lied. I keep my money, and next fall I'll enter Oberlin College!"

What other tricks do you have up your sleeve, Lucy? Because you're not getting there so soon on a small town reporter's salary.

CHAPTER EIGHT

With all the headlines Amelia Bloomer runs about woman's rights and husband horrors—not to mention the space she gives bloomer patterns—*The Lily* is hotter than a fart in a skillet. Lucy and me feel a big part of that success. Miz Bloomer, a hearty supporter of Lucy's college plans, wants her to be a writer. Thinks Lucy will end up some day in a big city—Rochester, Buffalo, maybe even Boston or New York—working for a big bug newspaper like the *New York Herald*. Lucy eats up the glory, so it surprises me sometimes when she turns glum and stays away from *The Lily* for a day or two. When she comes back, her eyes are red and squinty and her hands sore. I noticed long ago that her fingertips are brown and calloused and that seems strange for a rich gal. Sometimes she favors them and can barely hold a pencil to write her stories. Those days she looks like she hasn't slept much and is cranky and barks at everyone. Even me.

One day she doesn't come in and I cover her interview, collecting quotes from farmers about the drought. I decide to run by her house and see what she's up to. Katherine, the housekeeper, lets me into the foyer.

"Miss Lucy is upstairs in her room."

"I'll take you up." The little guy, Freeman, grins at me. He has some dark, sticky goop all around his mouth.

"No you don't, young man. You stay right down here. You know your sister doesn't allow you in her room." Katherine puts a hand on the back of his head and a wet rag to his mouth.

"Sometimes I sneak in there when she's not home," he whispers to me with a devilish grin. The kid's been taken under the wings of the Stanton boys and has honed a naughty streak.

"I really should announce you first," Katherine says.

"No, you're busy. I'll just go up. Which door?"

"Second on the right."

I chuck Freeman under the chin and mount the stairs, walking carefully so they don't creak. I'm not sure why I want to sneak up on Lucy, but

I do. She has something going on besides *The Lily* and I want to know what it is. I don't knock. Just turn the doorknob and step in.

"AAAHH!" Lucy shrieks like she's been scalded.

There's a flurry of motion. She grabs at stuff on her bed, jams pieces of something into a bag, reaches for this and that and things start falling on the floor. Hard things like scissors and boxes of pins that THUNK and CLANG. Spools of thread roll across the wide oak planks.

"Calm down, Luce. What the heck you doing?"

"Tess!" She lays a trembling hand over her heart. "Tess. Oh, my…"

"What the heck's wrong with you?"

Feet stomp up the stairs. Lucy waves frantically for me to shut the door. "Don't let them in!"

I stick my head outside the door. "It's okay. I just surprised her." Katherine tries to peek around my wide shoulders and the little snipe Freeman tries to push between my legs. "She was napping and I scared her. Sorry about that. My fault." I close the door on them and walk to Lucy's bed.

"What're you doing, Luce? What is all this?"

Blood drips from her fingertip. She looks at me with tired eyes and wraps a handkerchief around her finger. I start picking things up off the floor. After I've collected two pairs of scissors and several spools of different colored thread, I stand, hands on hips, waiting for her explanation.

She laughs softly. "Well, you found me out. Now you know how I'm paying my way to Oberlin."

"What're you making?"

She pulls some fabric shapes out of the bag. "Gloves. My friend Charlotte got me a job at the factory in town. I work at home, and my father does not know, so please, *please* do not tell a soul!"

"Does your ma know?"

"Yes. I told her years ago."

"You've been doing this for *years*?" I sit down on the edge of the bed.

"Yes. I must. *I'm stitching my way to Oberlin*," she sings gaily, but her eyes are rimmed with tears and I'm not sure from fear or exhaustion. "I'm earning money. But unlike Charlotte's other friends, who hand every cent over to their husbands or fathers, no questions asked, I'm keeping my money. I've earned it. It's mine. And I'm going to use it to pay for college."

Lucy stacks glove shapes into piles, her hands still shaking. "I thought you were Freeman. He's such a snitch. He'd run straight to Father." She watches me carefully. "Tess, I know I'm not always nice to you."

I shrug. "We get along fine."

"Yes, now, but in the beginning I was rude."

"Snotty."

She laughs. "Yes, definitely snotty." She looks me straight in the eye. "But if Father finds out…"

"Cripes, Luce, do you think I'd tell him? I can't stand the old grouch. The way he treats you…and your ma."

Lucy shrugs. "Actually, the odd thing is he's not that unusual. He doesn't really do anything to hurt me. He provides well and doesn't deprive us of anything…"

"…he thinks you need. But if he thinks you don't need it, you don't get it."

"Correct. But I don't think other fathers are any different. Not those of my former classmates and certainly not those among Father's friends." She pauses. "It's what he doesn't think I need that I want most."

"What's that?"

"To be treated like a person. Why do men act like women aren't people?"

"Forget men. Forget them all. Miz Bloomer supports you. She thinks you'll end up at the *Herald* someday."

"Yes, but why do I have to abandon my family to do it?" She rearranges the glove shapes according to color. "If I go to college…"

"*When* you go to college."

"…Father will likely disown me."

I shrug. "Maybe not. He backed down about *The Lily*. And anyway, did he say you couldn't go or…?" I cock an eyebrow.

Lucy's face brightens. "That's right! He said he *wouldn't pay for it*! Tess, that's perfect. He'll have no control. It will be my money, my decisions."

"Sounds like a better deal to me." I glance at Lucy's brown fingertips. "But you're paying a big price. How much you get for those gloves?"

"Forty cents a pair. I just took in thirty pairs—snuck them out of the house—and received $12." She smiles like it's a fortune.

"So, after a few years you must have quite a stash. Hope you have a safe hiding place."

"Yes, I…"

"Don't tell me. Don't tell anyone." I smile. "You're good at working toward a goal, Lucy."

"I must! I can't end up like Mother. Dependent."

"You're secret's safe with me." I turn to go. "And if you ever need help sneaking gloves out of the house, let me know. I'm a really good sneak." I pause with my hand on the doorknob and watch Lucy rise from her bed, sit down in a straight-backed chair by the window, and pick out a glove shape cut from fabric. Taking out her needle, she carefully threads it and leaning ever so slightly into the light, begins to stitch. Tiny, patient stitches. One by one. Following in a line. All around the glove.

CHAPTER NINE

One day Miz Bloomer complains that the news and press rooms are cluttered, and I talk her into hiring Beany to tidy up the floors. Convincing Amelia was easy, but it's work getting August to let her precious Bean out of the house, out of her sight.

After Miz Bloomer puts the paper to bed, she teams up with Rebecca Harrington (always a big Beany supporter), and the two of them sandwich August in the kitchen. Miz Bloomer tells her this is a great opportunity for Beany. Says she can start out sweeping *The Lily* floors, run errands—but August stops her right there. Her Beany won't be running around town in broad daylight. No, ma'am. Not safe. So, Miz Bloomer nixes the errands quick and says with Beany being such a quick learner someday she might write something for the paper. That shocks even me.

Of course, August acts like they're trying to steal her baby, shaking her head and saying no, no, no. They finally wear her down when Miz Bloomer says she'll pay the Bean real money. August doesn't get squat as our cook. Most of her reward for slaving in the hot kitchen morning, noon and night, plus doing everybody's dirty laundry, is room and board, although the great Abner Manning tosses her maybe a dollar a week extra. Miz Bloomer says she'll pay Beany fifty cents. That's a big increase in their income.

Beany doesn't say boo the whole time Miz Bloomer talks to her ma, but I know the gal wants out. Beany ain't a kid anymore. Thirteen-year-old girls—even colored ones—get tired of being holed up in a hot kitchen in a tumble down boarding house day and night. I want to see the world. Beany will be happy to see Seneca Falls.

Goofy thing is, after she gets the job, Beany's stumped about what to do with her money. She tries giving it to August, but her ma says, no, you worked for that money, Beany, it's yours. I tell her to find a good hiding place. Maybe bury it in the backyard, but she's scared Pa'll find it and booze it. So, I don't know what the Bean does with her loot.

Lucy, now, she quick tucks her pay envelope right into her pocket. Doesn't take anything out for herself, not even a penny for a pretzel. She's hoarding hers and I know why.

I have a safe spot for my money in the loft. No one ever goes up there. Pa drags himself to the bottom half of the barn once in a while, looking for wood or nails when Boss Manning sets him on some handyman job. But I'm not worried. Pa gets in and out quick, taking as little time as possible at real work.

It isn't a secret what I save for either. Just about everything I earn is traveling money. Soon as I get completely fed up with Pa and Seneca Falls—soon as the printing ain't fun anymore—I'll be gone. The canal is right at my back door. I'm sixteen, grown, and ready to see the world!

Though she lets Beany go to *The Lily* every day, August is still queasy without her. Ma says if Beany isn't home by four o'clock August frets like a hen with one chick. And it isn't just because August wants help with supper. She convinces herself Beany's been stolen. Ma says she heard August praying out loud the slave catchers don't come to town.

Despite her brooding, Saturday is a great day for August, because Beany comes home with a present. She knew better than to ask me for help picking it out. Instead she asked if I thought Lucy'd help her.

"Well, ask her. She won't bite. She likes you."

"She does?" Like it's hard to believe.

"Yeah! Doesn't she call you that dumb name you and Miz Harrington picked out? Cottonwood? Honeysuckle?" Beany gives me a withering look. She's getting better at it. Everyone calls Beany "Willow" at *The Lily*. She gets paid real money and everybody calls her a pretty name. Everybody except me.

On Friday, Beany gives Lucy money to pick out something in the general store. Beany points through the window at the one she wants. Walking home, she clutches that package like the cloth inside is spun from gold.

August just about wakes snakes when Beany gives it to her. She's in the kitchen humming her favorite tune and chopping carrots with that sharp blue stone knife, when we walk in. Beany hands her the package.

"What that?"

"Open it, Mama." Beany grins like a cat.

"Why?"

"Because it's for you!"

"What in it?"

"A present."

"What?"

"A surprise!"

"Sweet Jesus, August! Open it." I flop down in a kitchen chair.

She snaps the brown twine with her knife—waves it at me for cussing—wraps it around her fingers then stuffs it in a drawer near the sink.

"Lordy, August, open the dang box!"

She pushes aside the wrapping and squeals.

"Beany...for me? You bought your Mama a new dress?" August can't say much more. She doesn't even scold the Bean for wasting money. She just hugs her and her face gets wet and her nose starts running. She squeezes Beany tight. Lordy, she loves that girl. And Beany sure loves her mama.

The dress is white with small purple flowers. August says it's the first brand new dress she's ever owned. Now, she wears it every Sunday afternoon, sitting out under the willow tree, sipping iced tea. Soon as she got that dress, she chopped off most of her long, stiff hair and now what's left curls around her face like a soft cap. Her black eyes sparkle in the sunshine and she looks like an African queen in one of Miz Harrington's books.

Beany usually sits on the grass and reads. Sometimes I hang around, catching snips of their conversation. Sometimes, August tells Beany slave stories, and later Beany writes them down in that flowery handwriting she's so proud of.

It looks to me like August and Beany have finally reached a point in their miserable lives when things are looking up.

CHAPTER TEN

We're quite the sight walking down Washington Street from *The Lily*, me and Lucy, and it makes me laugh out loud.

"What's funny?"

"Nothin'." But I chuckle again, because Lucy's tiptoeing along in a pretty summer dress, straw hat and reticule, while I slouch along in cutoff overalls, a cotton shirt and bare feet—I take my shoes off as soon as I leave the pressroom. I'm on my way to watch those Stanton boys while their ma bakes pies for the church bazaar. Lucy's going home to sew gloves, secretly.

Neal, Kit and Gat greet me in their front yard, holding out dirty hands, showing me nails and bugs and stuff. Lucy goes inside and as soon as her front door closes I hear it.

"LUCY!"

I shush the boys and cock an ear toward the Manning house.

"LUCY!" Her old man shouts. Prob'ly hollering from that dark library he likes to hole up in.

"Yes, Father?" I know by her shaking voice that Lucy's heart is beating like a circus drum.

"COME HERE IMMEDIATELY!"

"You boys go in the back yard and hunt up your fishing poles and dig some worms. I'll be along in a minute." They start to whine, but I scowl, threaten to go home if they argue, and they scat. I creep up to the side of the Manning house with the library window and peek inside.

Abner Manning is standing like a granite statue beside the fireplace, holding a cloth bag in the palm of his hand. I can't see Lucy.

"Close the door."

She walks slowly up to his wide desk and I see her shudder, like she's being threatened with a knife. "That's mine." Her voice trembles. The bag is fat and I know what's in it.

Manning bounces the bag in his big hand. "This is a bag full of money."

"How did you get that?" Lucy words ooze out like she's being strangled slowly.

"Freeman gave it to me."

Like a flicking whip, Lucy lurches forward and slams her fists on the desktop. "That's my money!"

"An admission which raises the question—why?" Manning shouts back. "Why do you have a large bag of money? You haven't been saving quarters long enough to acquire this amount of cash!"

"Freeman stole it from me!" Even I know that's not the answer he wants. Lucy puts one hand on her heart, the other on her throat. Is she choking?

"Thief! He stole my money!" When she screams the hair on my arms stands right up. Lucy raises tight fists to her forehead. "I won't lose it. I won't lose everything!"

"Where did you get this? Answer me!" Manning stretches across the desk like a hungry lion.

Lucy begins to pace. She waves her hands in front of her eyes, like she's brushing things away—needles, thread, fabric, patterns? Suddenly, coins bounce across the desktop. A few paper bills balance in the air then sift to the floor. Manning shakes the bag. Coins fall like hailstones. Lucy's hands sweep across the desk, rushing to gather them. Nickels and dimes spin wildly past her outstretched fingers and tinkle to the floor.

"I earned it! I earned this money!" she screams, swiping at the rolling coins. "I work! I sew! In my room! This is my money! Freeman's a thief!" She leans across the desk, snatching at dollar bills threatening to fly away forever.

Manning drops the bag and grabs Lucy's flailing hands. Stretching her across the desk, he holds them in front of his eyes. Rubs her tiny fingertips with his big thumbs. Rubs again. Back and forth. Lucy's face is white, bloodless and slick with tears. Her breath shoots in short puffs.

"How long have you been doing this?"

Lucy's head sinks below her outstretched arms. "A long time." She tries to pull away, but he holds her.

"Why do you need money, Lucy?" He asks sternly, but not in the angry bellow that summoned her to the library. She doesn't answer right away.

"I must go to Oberlin," she says finally and falls across the desk, sobbing. Manning releases her hands and stands as still as a stone watching her cry. Watching her cry. Watching her cry. Then he comes around, lifts her from the desk and steers her to a large-backed chair near the fireplace. Lucy slumps into the seat, and I wish the chair's wide wings would close around her like one of Ma's protecting angels. Manning walks to a corner table and comes back with a glass he presses into her hand.

"Drink this. It will calm you."

Lucy takes a sip. What's he giving her? Wine? Whiskey? Manning sinks into a leather chair with his glass. They sit, silent, and sip. The Stanton boys march up with pails and poles, but I make a face, shake my fist and send them off toward the river. I look back inside the library. Lucy stares unblinking at the desk where her money lays scattered.

Manning sighs wearily. "Your room is on the north side of the house. It's dark. Even during the day."

Lucy takes a big swallow from her glass. "I have...a small lamp on...my nightstand."

He sips. "I've noticed your eyes are often red."

Sip. Silence.

From the window I see his thick chest heave another sigh. "How much do they pay you?"

"Forty cents a pair." Sip.

Sip. "How many pairs have you sewn?"

"Hundreds."

Cripes, if her old man takes this loot, how will Lucy ever…?

Manning rubs his big hand across his forehead, scratches his eyebrows, massages his eyes. Lucy takes a long, slow sip from her glass. She sags deeper into the chair. He must have given her that stuff rich women drink. Miz Stanton has some. Sherry. Lucy's head slides against the side of the chair. When Manning speaks, she jumps.

"I will punish Freeman for invading your room and taking your money."

I watch another minute then walk off to find the boys near the river.

CHAPTER ELEVEN

When I watch her brats, Miz Stanton always feeds me—on top of what she pays me—so I'm not hungry when I get home, but start up the back steps anyway to see what Beany and August are up to.

"What'd you say when you found him snooping around Tessie's stuff, Mama?"

I stop dead and listen.

"Why, I so surprise to see him up there. I on top of the ladder and when he turn around I almost tumble down."

I look through the screen. August is washing and Beany drying a mountain of cooking pots.

"*What you doing up here?* he say, real mean-like. I say Miz Riley send me look for Tess. He have this little metal box, look like old tea box, in his hand. And a big grin on his face. Everything in that loft is topsy-turvy. Even some boards pull away from the walls."

My stomach turns rock hard and my fists roll into tight balls.

"Tess is always bragging how she's got her money hid good. Nobody'd ever find it. You think he found it, Mama?"

Me and Lucy. Both of us hit by thieves.

"That box rattle when he shake it. I know I shouldn't, but I ask him if that Tessie's money. Me thinking, poor Tess, she work hard."

Me and Lucy. On the same day.

"He snap like a swamp turtle. Tell me to shut pan. Say to get my butt off that ladder before he bust me up again. I scared, so I climb down and come back to the house."

"You gonna tell Tess he stole from her?"

My heart bangs against the front of my chest.

"I don't know, honey. He prob'ly drink it all up by now. Why tell Tessie?"

Miz Stanton's supper churns in my stomach. Plots for revenge punch inside my skull.

"She's gonna find out anyway, next time she goes to that tin can. And she should be mad, Mama! He robbed her!"

"I know, I know, Beany...but he the man, he the boss."

"He's the thief!"

I lean against the doorjamb. Beany sees me and I know she wants to snitch.

"Go ahead, say it, Bean."

"Somebody took your money, Tessie."

August spins from the sink. "Shut pan, girl! Never mind her, Tess."

I don't shout. Don't tear out of the house and up to the barn to see for myself, because I believe her.

"Beany! Why you talk! Stupid girl!" August looks to slap her. She doesn't know I've heard the whole rotten thing.

"There be too much trouble from this. Too much trouble." August looks at me like I'm dangerous and slaps at Beany with the wet dishcloth. "You make big trouble, girl." She sits down at the table and drops her head onto her arms.

Without a word I turn from the back door and walk down to the canal.

CHAPTER TWELVE

It's easy getting three towpath toughs—canal buddies of mine—to snatch Pa on his way out of Mallory's rum-hole. Two hold him while the third beats the snot out of him. I watch from around the corner. I tell them to search him first, and if they don't find any money to sock him extra hard. They don't find one penny.

The sot's drunk it all. Forty bucks of my hard-earned cash down his gullet. I hear about it later in town. Drinks around for his stinking booze buddies. Lost it all on liquor and cards. All my traveling money.

But he paid for it. My pals say they busted his nose and a couple ribs. Knocked out a front tooth. I watch him lay in an alley all Saturday night and half of Sunday 'til some kids find him.

I tell Ma he robbed me, but say nothin' about the beating. When Constable Parker helps him to the back door, she says, "Take him away. I don't want him here." He doesn't show up at home for another week.

I give Cooper the whole story in a letter, and he says he'll take me away this time for sure. Says he'll be in Seneca Falls in a couple weeks. Since the theft, I've saved every penny from *The Lily* and from the Stanton job, but it ain't squat compared to what I had and lost.

Today, I sit on our saggy back porch, enjoying the treasured picture of Pa's busted face and cracked teeth. August and Beany cozy up under the willow. Its long branches hide them except when a hot breeze blows the fronds aside. August is wearing that pretty purple and white dress that makes her black skin shine like polished stone.

She must be telling Beany old stories, because, when the branches part, I see her head hanging low. She's wearing that sad, telling-slave-stories-in-the-kitchen look. Not quite teary because she doesn't want the Bean to bawl. Beany knows what her ma's feeling, anyway. Those two are attached at the heart.

"THERE SHE IS!" Pa's voice jabs an old wound. "We got you now, black August! Don't run, nigger gal!" Here he comes on the run with two scraggy men behind him.

August screams a blood-chilling "NO!" Jumping up, she pulls Beany to her feet, but the kid, confused, only half rises and August drags her on her knees toward the side yard that leads to the street.

"GET HER, BOYS!"

I leap off the porch, tackle a guy with a red eye patch, and we roll through a flower bed. As we tumble, I see the other slave catcher, a big guy with huge hands, grab August and push her to the ground. Pa grabs Beany.

"LET ME GO!" Beany twists and stomps his feet and kicks his shins, but he grabs her around the neck, crushing her against his chest. Beany's strangled wails turn to, "Let her go. Let Mama go!"

"Shut up!" There's a loud slap.

I untangle myself from the one-eyed slaver and run toward August. She's rolled up in a ball, protecting against the big guy kicking her in the side. I jump in the air, boot him hard in the back and he collapses. Then I pick up August and run through the willow curtain shouting, "FIGHT, BEANY, FIGHT!"

I feel a hard punch between my shoulder blades and my lungs empty. Then One Eye socks me in the head with his fist. I hit the dirt and roll slowly away from the mess under the willow, clutching my chest.

Gasping for breath, I turn over and see Big Slaver's dirty boot on August's cheek, pushing her head into the ground. One Eye kneels on her back, twisting her arms behind her and tying her wrists with a thin, dirty cord. White spots dance before my eyes, and I fight not to pass out.

"We got you, nigger," One Eye says, wiping spit off his lips with a filthy hand. "Your running days are over. You're going home sweet home. South! They're waiting for you." He laughs wickedly. As I struggle to sit up, Beany's pathetic "Mamaaaa," is an eerie wail on a sluggish summer wind.

Ma runs out of the house, screaming at Pa to let Beany go, but he spits, swears and drags her toward the front of the house and Fall Street. Ma helps me to my feet, tries to hang on to me, but I pull away and stumble after them. I want to puke, can barely breathe, and my back hurts like the slaver sunk an ax into it. So does my head. I've tussled plenty with boys on the towpath but am stunned by the viciousness of these slave hunters.

When I reach the street, I see Miz Manning, Miz Bloomer and Lucy on the other side. Their smiles fade as they turn slowly toward the sound of Beany's pitiful wail. They and other Sunday Christians enjoying the afternoon sunshine gape at the two filthy men hauling a torn and beaten colored woman up the street toward the jail.

"Oh, my!" Miz Manning exclaims. "Who...? Is that August?"

"And Willow!" Lucy cries.

"Who are those men?" Miz Bloomer is confused only a moment.

"Lordy no! Slave catchers!"

Eyes blurred with tears, I gasp for breath and stumble along, hating what I see. Pa holds Beany like a boy holds a snake. One hand squeezes her upper arm and the other grips a handful of her long, curly hair. Beany's head is pulled so far back she can't see where she's walking. Her tortured wails fly straight to heaven. She reaches out to touch her ma, yanked and dragged a few feet ahead of her, but the separation is too wide.

"Mamaaaaa," Beany bawls over and over.

"Release those people!" Miz Bloomer demands.

"Out the way!" Big Slaver yells. They push past her up the sidewalk. Sunday strollers ooze into the street to let them pass.

"Mr. Riley, what in heaven's name are you doing?" Miz Manning asks, hurrying alongside him, covering her face with a hanky. Pa smells like a pit of pus.

But Lucy grabs Pa's wrist. "Let her go!" She tries to break his grip on Beany's arm.

He squeezes tighter and shoves Lucy with his shoulder. "Git!" He yanks Beany's head to show his authority.

"Mamaaaaa."

"What are you doing, Mr. Riley?" Miz Manning repeats, helplessly, twisting her white handkerchief.

"Helping catch a nigger,' he hisses. He shakes Beany's head violently.

"Let her go, monster!" Lucy screams, kicking him in the shin. She kicks him again. Grabs his head. Scrapes her fingernails across his greasy scalp. He howls and cusses. Tries to kick back. Miz Manning pulls Lucy away. Miz Bloomer shouts at the two men shoving August, and they shout back. The Sunday walkers murmur and flow out of the way like birds in flight. I get my breath back slowly and walk a little faster.

"She's a slave—a runaway," One Eye growls over his shoulder. "She's going back south where she belongs."

Miz Manning orders Pa to let Beany go or he's fired, but Pa is bold on booze and stalks past.

Miz Bloomer begins talking to the crowd, calling people by name, begging them to help. A few shout to the slavers to release Beany and August. Then Miz Bloomer runs ahead to the jail and demands Constable Parker stop the capture, but he crosses his arms and shakes his head.

"You'll read about this in *The Lily*, Parker," she threatens, but he says nothin' illegal is going on.

"You write down that the law's being served, lady," Big Slaver yells. "We're just doing our job."

"Yeah, you read that law real good," One Eye says. His patch is a red sore on his face. "You can get in big trouble for buttin' in."

It feels like someone is poking inside my head with a knife, and pain shoots deep in my chest when I breathe, but I walk fast enough to pull up alongside Beany. She twists her head to look me in the eye. Neither of us wastes energy on words.

"That child...that child being handled so roughly...was born here in Seneca Falls," Miz Manning says. She's panting, too. "She is not a slave! She is free!" Miz Manning's bluffing. She doesn't know anything about Beany, but I give her credit for trying. She runs her handkerchief across her hot, red face then grips her sides with both hands. I know her whalebone is killing her. She staggers.

"Miranda, calm down." Abner Manning crosses the street quickly and puts his arm around his wife. He must have come from the collection of big bugs talking in the park.

"Do something," Miz Manning pants. "This is criminal. These slave catchers cannot kidnap this woman and her child. Help them!"

"What proof do you have these people are slaves?" Manning demands, blocking One Eye's path.

"Don't need proof," the weasel whines.

"It can't be your word alone!" Miz Manning declares. "You can't just pull people out of their homes."

"Here! You want proof? Here's proof!" Pa lets go of Beany's arm, reaches over and yanks up August's dress, revealing a thick, coarse mark on her thigh. The Sunday gawkers gasp.

"There's your proof. She's a branded slave. That's her owner's mark." A stinging silence falls over the crowd.

"Maybe she was freed," Miz Manning challenges, but the two slavers and Pa are already dragging August and Beany into Parker's office. "Abner, help them."

I know what I have to do. I take a shallow, painful breath and push through the jailhouse door.

"Get the hell out of here!" Parker barks. He reaches for me, but I punch his arm away, kick him in the leg. "You want to go to jail, you two-bit brat? Grab her!" He motions to One Eye, and the two of them wrestle me into a cell. I bite back a scream when the pain in my chest drops me to the floor. Parker slides the heavy door, and it bolts with a loud CHUNK.

Rolled in a ball on the hard cement, I watch Big Slaver throw August on a wooden cot in the cell next to mine and chain her to the wall.

Pa still has Beany by her hair and arm. "Please let Mama go," she begs. Her face is slick with tears and her voice ragged from crying, but she screams at Parker. "She didn't do nothin'. She don't belong in jail. Let her go!"

Pa shoves Beany inside with August. I expect her to run to her ma, but she stands in the middle of the cell, throws back her head and wails, loud keening cries I know can be heard outside.

"Shut that kid up. She'll have the whole damn town in an uproar. Too many damn abolitionists…" Parker glances at Manning, who's followed us inside.

"Sissy slave lovers don't scare me," One Eye growls. He raises his fist to Beany. "Shut up! I'll punch you flat."

"Don't you dare," Manning warns, stepping forward, but Parker butts in.

"Enough!" He slams the door on August and Beany. "She's chained, she's locked. She ain't going nowhere. So you guys scram and let this town settle down." He waves the slave catchers and Manning out of the cell block. Beany rushes to the cot and covers August with her small, trembling body. Wraps her arms around her mama's waist. With a snide look at me, Parker closes the door between the jail and office.

CHAPTER THIRTEEN

I crawl to the bars dividing our cells. I've never been in jail before. I don't like the loud CHUNK that signals the door bolting shut. I'm wounded but wound like a top, already thinking of escape. Beany, on the other hand, looks lifeless.

"Mama, they can't take you," she whispers between hiccupping sobs. "You're free. You're up north, now. For years and years."

August's hand—the one not chained to the wall—comes up slowly and strokes Beany's back. Then August sighs deeply, a low death sigh.

"Your papa bring me north, honey," she says, so quietly I have to hold my breath to hear.

"My papa?" Beany holds still.

"It an easy trip for awhile. No questions asked."

I sit up and grip the bars. I've never heard nothin' about Beany's pa, and I'm pretty sure Beany never has either.

"Did you run away? How could it be easy, Mama? You must have been scared and hungry."

"No, honey, it not like that. All doors open to a colored maid traveling with her white massa."

"*What?*"

"I say your daddy was my white massa."

Beany raises her head and looks at August's face. Her ebony face, much darker than Beany's milk chocolate. She lays her head back down.

"You always said your massa was mean as the devil," Beany mumbles into August's torn dress. The little purple flowers are brown with mud. August kisses her head.

"That the old massa. Yeah, he mean. Young massa, he kind. Gentle. Sweet like summer strawberries. When I tell him you growing inside me, he hatch a plan for us to escape. Say nobody stop us. They think me his servant. I ask, what about old massa? He don't know we lovers, your papa say. He gonna tell his daddy we going to Baltimore to see his college friends." August falls silent, strokes Beany's hair.

"Why didn't you ever tell me this?" Beany asks, but August doesn't seem to hear.

"But I afraid. Don't want to go. He say he don't want his baby growing up a slave. See, Beany, he love you." Beany cuddles closer. I poke my nose between the bars. They don't seem to know I'm here.

"So, we plan to escape. But old massa, he sick, and start relying on your papa more and more, give him one job after another. Buy this, sell that. We can't leave quick, like we want. We don't get to go 'til my belly start filling up. I have hard time hiding it. And I real scared then."

Beany scrapes at the mud on August's filthy dress.

"I say, Morgan—that your papa's name—you should take a man slave, too. I real scared people bother a white man and colored woman. So he take my brother Tyler, and off we go to Baltimore. Morgan right—nobody stop a white man with two slaves, and folks prob'ly think me and Tyler make the baby.

"We don't tell Tyler we escaping, and he don't get to wondering till Morgan decide to visit another friend in Philadelphia. Then, when we next cross into New York, he ask '*Massa Morgan, exactly how far north we going this trip?*' and your papa say, '*Tyler, once we get to Elmira, you can go as far north as you want.*' So, when we get to Elmira, Morgan and me go straight north to Jefferson. Tyler, he go west and we never see him again."

"That's sad, Mama, you never saw your brother again." Beany rubs her cheek on August's chest, then asks quickly, "Am I too heavy, Mama? Want me to get off?"

"No, honey. You lay right there. You feel real good." She strokes Beany's hair.

"Your papa say we gonna ride up Seneca Lake and take a little canal to the big canal, the Erie. Then we gonna take the Erie Canal all the way to Rochester. Then we gonna take a boat to Canada." August stops. Her breathing gets ragged.

"But you didn't." Beany raises her head.

"They kill your papa, honey." August chokes on the words. "With Tyler gone, it look bad, a white man traveling with a woman slave. And my belly getting bigger and bigger. Night before we gonna leave Jefferson, Morgan put me on that boat we gonna take up Seneca Lake. Say, '*Stay here, I just going into town to send a message to my friend in Rochester*'. He give me his knife. That pretty blue stone one I use every time I need something sharp."

I grew up watching August stroke that smooth blue stone with a sweet touch every time she pulls it out and every time she puts it away.

"Where's that knife now, Mama?"

"Constable take it. That big slaver say I try to cut him with it, but I never get the chance to pull it out."

Beany stiffens. "Would you, Mama?"

"What?"

"Cut those slavers?" August doesn't answer. "If you killed them, Mama, the white folks would hang you." They lay quietly.

"I ain't going back to that plantation." We're all silent and motionless for a while.

Finally, August stirs. "Yeah, guess he put my knife somewhere in there." She moves her head slightly toward the office where it's real quiet. Fat Parker's prob'ly sleeping.

"Tell me more, Mama. You stayed on the boat. Then what?"

August moans. "Well, I hear the story from the boatmen later. I wait and wait for your papa to come back, but he don't. I wait all through the night, getting more and more scared. Now it daylight. That boat ready to leave.

"We can't go, I say, scared to be talking to the captain. My massa not back. We can't leave without him. They look at me, the captain and a boatman. They see me shaking. They look at my belly, too. Then the boatman say a white man killed last night. Maybe it my massa. I don't want to hear that. The captain send the man to check. He come back, say, yeah, Morgan killed and dumped in the lake."

Beany breaks into sobs and August holds her close. "Why'd they kill him, Mama?"

"Oh, the usual trouble, honey. Some men start sassing him. They see your papa with me when they load their boat. They start saying maybe I more than a maid. They circle Morgan and taunt him. Poke him. Try to rile him. Morgan don't want to fight, the boatman say, and I know that true, because he know I waiting for him. And he don't have a weapon. They follow him and beat him up bad. One stab him with a long knife. And dump him in the lake."

They lay quietly, August smoothing Beany's hair, Beany stroking August's shoulder and giving her little kisses wherever her lips touch.

"You were all alone, Mama. What'd you do?" Beany speaks so softly, I can barely hear her.

"I don't know what to do. I want to go find your papa, but the captain say '*Stay away from there. Your massa dead, and those men maybe cut you open and pull that baby inside you right out!*' That scare me so bad, because I believe there ugly men evil enough to do such a horrible thing.

"The captain ask if Morgan have money. I say, yeah, in his trunk. The captain say if I give him the money, he take me to a village called Geneva.

So I give it to him. Still, he make me cook and clean his cabin. He want more than just a cook, too. Say he run his boat up and down Seneca Lake and want a friend along for company.

"But I don't want no strange man jumping all over me—and you—so I sneak off that boat in Geneva and walk east for days in the bushes and weeds along the towpath, but only at night. It hard stealing along alone, watching for dogs. Hoping I don't come across somebody sleeping in the weeds. In the daytime I hide in the woods. I getting awfull hungry and so thirsty, but I afraid to steal out of people's gardens.

"Then one morning, I come to a big house with a long porch across the back. My stomach growling and a powerful thirst scratch at my throat. I dirty and worn out. And I worried sick about you, not getting any food or water for so long. So, I shake up my courage and sneak up to the back door. Inside I hear singing. A sweet voice. Then I hear a racket. Little kid noise. Yelling and banging—something pounding on a tabletop. The singing stop and the nice voice tell the kids be quiet, eat their breakfast. I come closer. Tap on the door, hand shaking, loud enough, I hope, for the lady to hear through the racket.

"I hear a little kid yell '*Ma! Ma! Somebody at the door!*'."

"I tap again, and when the door open, I fall back. I just asking for a cup of water, missus, I say, my eyes on the porch floor. Just a little water, then I be gone. The lady stare at me with big, dark eyes. Maybe she never see a colored woman before. I hear chairs scrape and then two little faces watch me. Little boy face, little girl face. Then that lady come down the step, take my arm and bring me into the kitchen and sit me down at the table. '*Cooper, Tessie, sit down*', she say, and the children hop right up, better to get a look at me, I guess."

"That was Coop and Tess?" Beany lifts her head. I feel strange figuring in a story I've never heard before. Not even from Ma.

"Yeah, it them." A tiny laugh escapes like a miracle from August's bloody lips. "Cooper six years old, maybe. Tess a few years younger."

"So...that was our boarding house? I was born here? Not on a canal boat?"

"You born right in that little room off the kitchen, because Miz Riley let me stay. Say she been thinking of getting some hired help. Say if I can cook, I can stay. I say sure I can cook, and it ain't no lie, because a house slave like me cook for big parties and holiday dinners besides everyday suppers."

"Riley was there, too, Mama?"

"'Course he there, honey. He father those two babies."

I press my forehead into the cold steel bars and my mind clouds with hate. Pa siring me is dark mark on my soul.

"Was he a drinker back then, too?"

"Yeah, he always a drinker. But Miz Riley stand up to him when he say '*Get that nigger out of this house!*' She go to Mr. Hurley and tell him she find a cook, and he say good. Then she tell her husband Mr. Hurley know all about the new cook."

"Did he find out you were colored?"

"Oh, yeah. I cook there a few weeks when he come to dinner. I remember him sitting at head of the table and when one of the mill girls complain something missing, Miz Riley ring that little bell, and I come out. I feel Mr. Hurley's eyes on me, but he don't say nothin'. Well, all I hear him say is '*Fine dinner, Mrs. Riley*' as I leave the dining room."

"Miz Riley's good to us."

"Yeah, honey, she a kind woman. Help me birth you. Clean you off. Cradle you like you her own baby." Then August laughs. I can't believe she's in jail chained to a wall and laughing. "And Tessie banging on the door, yelling '*Mama! Mama! I wanna come in!*'" My face gets hot against the cold bars. "That Tessie always a bold one."

"Too bad she's locked in jail with us."

"*What?*" August turns her head and sees me on the floor. "What you doing here, girl?"

"I'm gonna get you out."

August laughs and waves her hand.

Beany looks over her shoulder at me. "Can you get Mr. Manning to help us?"

"Aw, he can't help me, honey." August wraps a curl around Beany's ear.

"Lucy says he's a powerful lawyer. Maybe he can keep them from taking you back south." August doesn't say anything. "Mama, you always say you're never going back to no plantation."

August starts humming. "Yeah, that what I say, baby. I ain't never going back to no plantation. That the truth."

"So, someone has to get you out of jail."

"I guess so." She sounds far, far away.

The door between the office and cellblock opens and the fat constable waddles in, followed by One Eye. Parker opens the door to August's cell.

"What you want?" I struggle to my feet and grab on to the steel bars separating me from Beany. The pain in my chest is knife-hot.

"Shut up, girly boy."

When One Eye reaches down and grabs Beany by her hair, August starts to howl.

"Leave her alone!" I kick at the bars with my heavy brogans.

"What's the name of your plantation in Maryland?" Parker asks, licking a pencil. August pulls on the chain, looks at him wild-eyed, then at Beany.

One Eye raises his hand, brings it down fast and hard on Beany's face. She cries out and clutches her cheek.

"Stop it, stinking horse shit!" I shriek.

"Merrywood!" August yanks on the chain. "Merrywood. Please don't hurt my girl!"

One Eye swings again and blood splatters out of Beany's nose onto her chin. Crying out in pain, she covers her face with one hand and grips One Eye's hand on her hair with the other.

"Leave her alone!" I kick the bars again.

"Stop! Please!" August turns on the cot, her arm twisted behind her.

"And what's the name of your owner?"

"Massa Stevens. Don't hit her, please. Massa Stevens!"

One Eye swings his arm back and plasters a hard slap on Beany's forehead. She dangles from his hand, dazed.

"Hey, man, she answered the question." Parker frowns. "You didn't have to do that."

One Eye shrugs and drops Beany on the floor. Stunned, she crawls across the stones and climbs awkwardly onto the cot. August clutches her to her chest.

I spit at One Eye and pray to Ma's God I have a chance to get him back.

CHAPTER FOURTEEN

Around suppertime, Lucy shows up with her ma and pa and Miz Stanton's husband, Henry. Her face is blotchy, her eyelids puffy. Manning carries a large book.

"Willow. August." Lucy presses her face against the bars. Neither of them seem to hear her. Lucy sees me sitting cross-legged on my wooden cot and motions me closer. "Are they badly hurt?"

I tell her August's right eye is swollen shut and her upper lip is split to her nose. I don't know what Beany's face looks like, but it has to be ugly. I look over Lucy's head at Henry Stanton and the Mannings standing near the door, whispering. Lucy turns and follows my gaze.

"Father, do something! You can't let those slave catchers collect a reward for stealing Willow's mother!"

"August has been here for years, Abner," Miz Manning says. "Surely, she's a free woman."

"Absolutely not!" Manning exclaims. "She is not a free woman. You know that, Miranda. She is an escaped slave and according to the Fugitive Slave Act must be returned to her rightful owner." Like all rich folk, they talk in front of underlings like we aren't even here.

"Her *rightful owner*? Abner!"

"Those aren't my words. I didn't write the law. I'm against slavery—but there's nothing I can do about this."

I stagger to the front of my cell. "You're gonna let those creeps take August away? Look what they did! Beany show them your face. Turn around! Show them!" Beany buries her head deeper into August's shoulder.

"What happened?" Miz Manning asks, approaching the bars.

"Parker let that one-eyed slave catcher hit her—three times—to make August tell him the name of her owner and the plantation she lived on. She gave the names fast, but he still bloodied Beany."

"Abner, call the doctor."

"No doctor will come to this jail today," Henry Stanton says gruffly. "And I'm afraid the mother's a lost cause. It'll be all we can do to stop them from taking the little girl."

"No! Not Willow!" Tears spill down Lucy's cheeks.

"She's the daughter of a slave. That makes her a slave. They'll try to take her, too."

"She was born in this town," I shout. "I know that for a fact!"

Stanton shakes his head sharply. "That doesn't mean anything. They'll still try to take her. And she'll probably want to go!" He raises his hands helplessly. "She'll want to go with her mother."

"No! She's not going! You do something!" I yell through the bars. "Or do you just hold meetings and sign petitions? That's all crap. Help her! If you don't you're nothin' but liars! Fakers!"

I scream and kick in frustration, but other feelings—regret, shame—burn me like a branding iron.

There's commotion in Parker's office, and Cooper—tall, muscular and golden-skinned—throws open the door to the cellblock and stalks in, fists balled.

"Tess!" He sticks his arms through the bars and holds me. His body is thick from lifting cargo. I cling to him, fighting to control the whirl of emotions spinning inside me.

"Ma said you were here. Parker wouldn't let her in. She said Pa turned August in to slave catchers." He calls into the cell next to mine. "Don't worry August, we'll get you out." She doesn't answer. She and Beany only see, hear and touch each other. Coop lets me go and faces the Mannings.

"I'm Tess's brother. Cooper." He shakes hands. "I sailed up Seneca Lake to Geneva with that scum. They didn't hide being slave catchers. They were in every gin joint in Jefferson, bragging how they'll be coming back down the lake real soon with a cargo of black cotton."

"They came looking for August?" I ask, stunned.

"Not her in particular. They were just sure they'd catch themselves some runaways. Said New York's full of 'em."

"But how'd they meet your father?" Lucy asks. Coop leans against the bars of my cell and crosses his arms.

"Soon as the boat docked in Geneva, they headed for the nearest groggery. That's where they met Pa. He was in Geneva, prob'ly because his credit's no good in most rum-holes around here."

"So...did you talk to him?" I stand as close to Cooper as the steel bars allow.

"I hitched a wagon ride from Geneva today. Came up just as they were pushing you all into the jailhouse...that devil Parker stepping aside to let them in. I saw him turn Ma away when she tried to follow.

"I sat off by myself 'til Pa came out. He was full of bluster, proud of what he'd done. Ready to brag, even to me. I got him away with a promise of some special liquor I brought from Buffalo. Got him drunk and he started telling his story.

"He said those two devils bought him a drink in Geneva then asked if there were any people of color in these parts. Pa said a few. They bought him another drink and asked if he knew where any were—exactly. He said two worked for him. They bought him a few more drinks and said they'd buy him his own bottle if he showed them where the slaves were. So he took them to our house." Sadness clouds Cooper's eyes. "And you know the rest."

We're silent until Lucy asks, "Father, isn't there any way around this horrible fugitive slave law?"

Manning finally opens the big book he's been clutching and starts reading about the law passed last September. He says it's a stricter version of the old Fugitive Slave Law passed sixty years ago. The new law says slave owners have a right to recover their property. Anyone can catch a runaway slave and collect the reward—$200. The slave catcher doesn't have to prove the colored person is a runaway slave. All he has to do is say he is. Or she is.

When threatened with capture, people of color can't fight to defend themselves. They don't get a trial by jury. Yeah, Parker can be fined $1,000 if he doesn't cooperate with the slave catchers. And anyone else who stands in the way of a bounty hunter, a slave catcher—anyone who interferes with a slave owner's *right* to recover his *property*—can be fined $1,000 and jailed for six months.

"So you can go to jail if you take serious action to help them?" Miz Manning asks.

"Yes," her husband replies. "So can you. So can Lucy."

Chicken shits! Who needs you? Coop and I will spring Beany and August. I'm surprised when Lucy pipes up.

"Whatever the consequences, we can't let them take August back to a plantation." She's wearing that same pig-headed look that used to rub me raw. She turns her back so August and Beany can't hear her whisper. "Father, you saw her back covered with scars. You know they'll whip her horribly when they get her back in Maryland. We must do something."

But all Abner the Abolitionist can do is read from his big law book. He takes his wife's arm and reaches for Lucy's, but she pulls away and stands next to Cooper in front of my cell.

"I'm staying."

Manning opens his mouth, then shuts it quickly and steers his wife out the door. Henry Stanton follows. As soon as they leave, Parker sticks his head through the doorway.

"You guttersnipes got five minutes."

"Drop dead, Parker." Coop glares and the lawman cusses under his breath but waddles back to his desk, leaving the door open.

Cooper runs a hand through his coppery hair. "Man, after all these years, Pa turns August in for a drink." Suddenly, the blister that's been throbbing inside me swells and pops.

"It's my fault!" My body sags against the bars. "Pa turned on August because I had him beat up for stealing my traveling money! I had to get even. Then he took revenge."

"You beat up your own father?"

My face flushes red hot. I'd forgotten how much I hated Lucy's haughty tone. Or how she could look down her nose at me—disgusted.

I strike back. "An eye for an eye!"

"And look at the consequence!" Lucy's tear-filled eyes are raw with disbelief.

But Coop's sympathetic. "It ain't your fault, Tessie." He rubs my shoulder through the bars. "Beat up or not, Pa would tell on August easily for a drink. They caught him when he was ripe. He's a mean drunk. And when he's sober, he's just mean." His words don't make me feel any better.

We hear the springs under Parker's wooden chair scream in protest when he sits down. If Lard Belly falls asleep, we can get something going.

Lucy edges over to Beany's cell. "Willow? *Willow.*" Beany lifts her head off August's chest and looks at us with tortured eyes. One half of her face is bruised, her lip split. Lucy motions her to the bars, but Beany doesn't move.

"We need to know where you were born, Willow...some sort of proof."

"Oh, shut pan," I growl. "Proof? She ain't got nothin'." I slide to the floor and press my forehead against the cool bars. Did Lucy think August kept a diary of her travels? Or registered Beany's birth with the town clerk? Stupid girl! How had I ever liked her?

"How long do they have to stay in here?" Coop calls to Parker.

"Until I hear from her owner. See if he really has a slave missing, matches her description."

"She doesn't have an *owner*," Lucy snaps. Parker laughs.

"And mind you, I didn't have to send that telegraph," he calls smugly. "Law doesn't say I need proof before those slave catchers can haul them away. I'm just doing it to satisfy your old man, missy. Keep that big bug off my back."

Coop rubs his chin thoughtfully then pounds one fist into another. "No more standing around," he hisses. "We're gonna get them out of here. Parker!" he calls. "When's the last time they had food or water?"

When there's no reply, Lucy peeks through the doorway. "I can't believe he's asleep already, just like that."

"Let's bust 'em out!" I grip the bars.

"No. Not yet," Cooper says. "Still light out. Those two slavers won't go far until they get word from that plantation owner."

"And if she isn't...isn't his?" Lucy chokes on the last word.

"Well, they won't forget her, that's for sure. Parker will let August go, but those slavers will snatch her again and take her south without bothering with lawmen next time. They'll try to sell her. Beany, too."

"So we gotta bust 'em out!" I kick the bars.

"Uh, wait...you're not..." Lucy's voice trembles.

"Shut up!" I push at her through the bars. "Chicken shit."

"How...how can you?" Lucy rubs her forehead, confused, spreads her hands. "You can't ... he'll hear you."

"Shut up or go home!" I surge with energy. "What's the plan, Coop?" He chews his lower lip. "You got a plan?"

Coop's eyes rest on each of us. He nods once. I smile.

The plan is simple. Parker is snoring like a sick elephant, so Coop and Lucy sit with us 'til twilight. Then Coop hides her among the coats and boots in the large closet behind Parker's desk and leaves the jail. Parker—the fool—never hears a thing or moves a muscle.

And Lucy understands now. She doesn't fuss. She knows, like Coop knows and I know, that this is Beany and August's only chance.

CHAPTER FIFTEEN

Coop's been gone more than an hour, and I bet Lucy's arms and legs are prickling with needles. Her old man hasn't come looking for her yet, surprising because it's dark outside, she's missed dinner and her folks must wonder where she is. I don't want old Manning screwing up the deal. Lucy should make her move soon.

I press against the bars and see her crack the closet door and peek out. Parker leans back in his chair, boots on his desk, snoring. After Coop left, he got up to lock the front door like we figured he would then collapsed back into dreamland.

Lucy opens the closet door quietly, sticks her head out and looks around the room. She glances at the wall clock. It must be about nine o'clock and I bet she'd rather be home sewing gloves. A small, nervous cough escapes her lips and my stomach flip-flops. She clamps a hand over her mouth. Parker stirs. Cripes! Shut pan, Luce, and unlock the front door!

Stretching the closet door just wide enough, she crouches low and duck-walks out. How the heck can she walk scrunched over like that in a skirt and corset? THUNK! Something in the closet tips over. Parker stirs again. Sweet Jesus! Beads of sweat slide down my temples.

Lucy waddles beside Parker's chair, near the keys dangling from a thick ring stuffed into his pants pocket.

"Mmmm...huh....unnn." Parker sighs and shifts to the left side of his baggy butt. Startled, Lucy tips over onto the floor and winces. Blood must be rushing through her crushed veins setting her legs afire. If Parker wakes up...can she run? Parker grunts, settles his shoulders. Lucy bites her lower lip, holds her breath.

What's this? A look of wide-eyed horror creeps across Lucy's face. The keys are moving! Sliding out of Parker's pocket. I hear the tinkle-tinkle of jail keys in motion, then see Lucy's right hand reach out and catch the ring. Her left hand comes up to silence the keys and there she sits, swaying back and forth. If Parker didn't hear those keys jingling like sleigh bells, maybe he won't hear Lucy's pounding heart.

Fighting her skirt and corset, Lucy rises to a half crouch. Clutching the key ring and grabbing fistfuls of fabric to raise her skirt above her shoes, she duck-walks to the front door and unlocks it, then continues her strange scuttle through the doorway that leads to our cells.

I give her a silent thumb's up. She scrinches her face, ready to bawl. I hold a finger to my lips. The worst is over, Luce. Now wait for Coop behind the door, like he told you.

"WAKE UP!

Parker lurches in his chair and shakes himself awake.

"How'd you get in here?" he mumbles. I watch through the doorway from the front of my cell.

"You left the door open," Coop says calmly, setting a sack on the jailer's desk. "Getting sloppy, Parker."

"I...I locked that." He reaches for Coop's sack. "You got food?"

"Hands off, lardbutt!"

"Watch your mouth, boy. I'll...." He stops and cocks his head. "What's that?"

Coop shrugs. "I don't hear nothin'."

"Tapping."

I see Coop cock his head, pretending to listen. Shrugs again. "Don't hear it."

Tap. Tap. Tap.

"KNOCK IT OFF!"

"Who you yelling at?" Coop laughs. "You think someone's chopping that chain off the wall?"

"Somebody in there?" Parker's boots pound toward the cellblock.

Tap. Tap. Tap.

"SHOW YOURSELF!" He barrels through the doorway, and I see his gun glint in weak moonlight slipping through the high jailhouse window.

BANG! Parker crashes onto the hard floor and lies still as dead dog. Coop holds the small black fry pan from the kitchen. Lucy appears slowly from behind the door, and Coop grabs Parker's keys from her shaking hand. The first one he tries opens my cell. Then he opens Beany's, and I pull her off the cot and hug her.

Jolted by the motion, August stirs. "What you kids doing?"

I let Beany go. "We're bustin' you out." I hold August's chain tight against the wall, and Coop starts swinging with a small, sturdy ax he pulls out of the sack. One, two, three, four whacks with the ax.

"Break. Break." I whisper.

Five, six, seven...

Beany sits on the floor, watching. August has her face turned away from the swinging.

Eight, nine, ten, eleven. Coop keeps swinging, not giving up.

"Someone's going to hear," Lucy whimpers, covering her ears.

"Shut up!" This is no time for cowards.

Twelve, thirteen. With a hard CHUNK the chain separates, and August's arm drops free.

"Let's go," Coop hisses, wiping sweat from his forehead. I turn his sack upside down. Some of Ma's hats and shawls fall out, and I put them on Beany and August.

"Parker took Mama's knife." Coop rummages through the constable's desk drawer then shoves August's pretty blue stone knife into his pocket.

"He still out?" Coop asks Lucy, who looks whiter than usual. She stares at Parker and shrugs.

I bump the constable with my foot. "Yeah, he's out."

Coop pulls Parker by his boots into the cell. He peers down at him, wiggles him a little then locks him in. I take Beany and August by the hands and lead them to the door. Neither says a word.

"Lucy, check the window," Coop orders. "Anyone coming?"

Eyes large as duck eggs, she squats in her whalebone, waddles to the window and looks out. "Don't see anyone." Her voice cracks with fear.

"Open the door. Check outside."

Trembling, Lucy opens it, sticks her head and shoulders outside, looks around then waves her hand for us to come.

Coop leads us onto the sidewalk. He closes the jail door, locks it, and we start walking. The street is empty. Silent. Pitch black.

"Where we going?" Beany asks, shivering despite the warm night. Cooper holds a finger to his lips, and we keep walking.

CHAPTER SIXTEEN

I slap my cheek and inspect my bloody fingers.

"Your face look like a popcorn quilt before this over." August waves at mosquitoes dancing around her swollen eyes. I feel the bumps on my forehead and cheeks. They match in size and itchiness the ones on my neck, arms and shoulders.

"Is anyone else getting bit like this?"

"No, princess, just you." Coop smacks his neck and grimaces.

"We left the princess behind," I grumble.

"Don't bad-mouth Lucy," Coop scolds. "She did her job. We couldn't have pulled it off without her."

"Yeah, then she chickened out." We hide in tall bushes just below the boarding house. A stupid place to hide. First place fat Parker will look is along the towpath. Right behind our own house! I want to walk farther, get out of town, but Coop says August is too beat up. He thinks her ribs are broken because her breathing is pained and ragged. My own chest twinges when I take a breath.

"Lucy can't come," Coop whispers. "She's not made for the canal. She's a lady."

"What, you sweet on her or something?"

He huffs and gives me the evil eye.

"Coop's right, Tessie. That little girl don't belong on the canal." I can barely understand August through her slashed lip.

"She's gonna snitch."

"She won't!" Of course Beany defends Miss Priss.

"Yeah, she will. Her pa'll get it out of her. Make her feel guilty. Shamed the family or some garbage like…."

"Don't talk like that," Beany whines. "You like Lucy. You're friends." She buries her head in her arms.

"Yeah, shut up, Tess." Coop throws a stone at my shoe. "She helped us. What more do you want?"

I don't want to be right here, right now. The annoying mosquito buzz—and the nasty gallnippers themselves—are getting under my skin, making me miserable. And I'm disappointed Lucy didn't come with us.

"We've been sitting here all night, Coop. When's your boat coming?"

He sighs wearily. "I told you. It leaves Geneva at daybreak. It'll stop here six-thirty, seven o'clock to pick me up."

"And you expect us to jump on board in broad daylight!"

"Yeah."

"Sakes alive, somebody'll see us! They must have found Parker by now. He's rounded up the slave catchers. Pretty soon they'll be crawling all over this towpath!" I knock over the small pile of rocks I've been building.

"I don't think Parker's awake, Tess."

"He can't still be out cold. Even Parker can't sleep that long."

Coop pauses. "I think he's cold as a wagon tire."

Three heads swing toward him. Coop stares at his hands. Runs his tongue over his lower lip. "He wasn't breathing when I dragged him into the cell."

August and Beany gasp.

"Oh! So now you killed somebody!" I throw a rock at him.

"Get the hell out of here then!" Coop throws a handful of dirt at me. "You don't have to stay."

"Yeah, I do!" I throw a handful back at him.

"All you do is complain. Go on, beat it!"

"And where do you think I can go?" Silence.

August's head slumps onto her chest. Beany stares at the water.

"Well, that's just it, right?" Coop snarls. "Ain't no place to go except on the canal. It's the best way out of Seneca Falls. Take it or leave it." I scowl. "Look, we don't have a wagon or horses. We can't walk, August's in too much pain. They'd catch us easily. This is the best way."

"Only if nobody sees us jump the boat—which I doubt."

Cooper swears and turns his broad back to me. Lord Almighty, he thinks he killed Parker!

"What makes you sure your captain will take us? All of us," I ask after Coop's shoulders relax.

"Captain Beale's a good man. A Christian man."

"Christian!" I snort. "That's something good in your book?"

"Tessie, please. Don't fight with Cooper. He trying to help us, best he can." I wish August wouldn't talk. It sounds too painful.

"We should hide in some hollow during the day. Hike out tonight when it's dark. I just don't like this daylight escape stuff."

August looks from me to Coop and shakes her head. "I'm sorry," she mumbles tearfully. She still has that chain hanging from a steel ring around her wrist.

"Don't be sorry." Coop shoots me a fierce look.

"You kids in bad trouble now. Bustin' me out of jail. Killing the constable." Tears make rivers down her dirty cheeks. Beany puts her arms around her mama, pulls August's head down to her shoulder.

"It's not your fault, August." It's my fault and guilt gnaws at my gut. "I want to get out of Seneca Falls anyway, right? Haven't I said that since I was little?" August buries her face in Beany's shoulder, and for a second they seem to reverse roles with Beany now the mama.

But Beany is still all white eyes and stony silence. Her face is filthy and peppered with bug bites. One eye, like her ma's, is swollen shut. She clings to August. August clings to Beany.

"Maybe we should walk west to Waterloo. Get farther away from Parker. Meet the boat before it gets to Seneca Falls and then they don't have to stop. Can sail right past this stupid town."

Coop groans. "It's too late for that, Tess. And dammit, listen! Parker's not gonna hurt us. He's not talking."

"Well, somebody must know August's gone by now. Soon as those slave catchers find out she's missing they'll..."

"They're still sleeping off hangovers."

"...be running all over town looking for her."

"But they're not looking for us! They have no clue who broke out August. And anyway, I know from experience, sometimes the best place to hide is right under somebody's nose."

"This is the first place..."

"Shut up!" Coop looks ready to slug me. "I'm sick of your whining! The boat's coming any minute. Stop bellyaching." I rest my head on my knees.

August lifts her head. "Hey, Coop, you got my blue stone knife?"

He reaches in his pocket. "Here you go."

August rubs her thumb over the deep blue stone and tucks it in her pocket.

"How are me and Mama gonna get to Canada, Tessie?"

I stretch my neck wearily. "That where you want to go?"

"That's where Papa said he was gonna take Mama before he got killed.

"We'll take you, Bean," Coop says softly. "We'll take this canal to the Erie, then the Erie to Rochester. Cross to Canada on a big boat."

"Your captain will let Mama and me on his boat?"

"Sure. He's a good man."

"Cripes, since when do you take faith in a Christian man?" Bitterness poisons my mood even further. I think back to the Christian men who stood at the church door to make sure August didn't cross the threshold at my baby brother's funeral. I remember Ma's priest who threatened to toss her out of church if she didn't take her husband back after he killed her baby son, still inside her. I know he's the same Christian man Pa gets drunk with every Saturday after confession. But it's the picture of all those Christian men strolling along Fall Street, who didn't lift a finger to rescue August and Beany from slave catchers that lights the anger behind my eyes most brightly.

Cooper swats another mosquito. "Captain Beale's a good man. Or else I wouldn't work for him."

Unconvinced, I watch August pull her knife from her pocket. She strokes the blue stone, opens the knife, picks up a maple leaf and slices clean through, no effort at all. Closes the knife. Strokes it. Puts it away.

Beany glances at me sideways with her good eye. The swollen one looks like it has a hen's egg under the lid. "I won't ever see Lucy again."

"Forget Lucy," I mumble.

"She helped Mama." Tears slide down her bruised cheeks. "What if the constable puts her in jail for bustin' us out?"

"Coop says Parker's dead. And he never saw Lucy anyway. Forget her. Worry about yourself, Bean, and your ma."

"I am worried about Mama—afraid those slave catchers are looking for us right now."

"We'll be on the boat soon." Coop scratches his bug bites.

"What if those slavers catch us first?"

"Coop and I won't let them hurt you...or your mama."

"Beany, honey," August says gently. "Don't worry. You gonna be okay. And I ain't gonna get caught. I ain't going back to no plantation, you can believe that."

"Mama, I'm scared." August wraps her arms around her girl and cradles her like a baby. Kisses her head, strokes her cheek and starts humming one of the little songs she sang in the kitchen. The same one she sang chained in jail. "It's gonna be okay, honey, okay, okay, okay."

"Boat's coming!" Coop jerks to attention, and we gulp at the sight of two sets of long ears bobbing past the bushes. The mules plod past our hiding spot, then the sleepy little hoggee, followed by the long lines that pull Coop's cargo.

CHAPTER SEVENTEEN

Coop's mouth opens round and wide and he yells something, but I can't hear. All I hear are hooves thundering, wheels skidding and BANG—a gunshot!

"THERE THEY ARE! GRAB 'EM!"

Coop yells again. "RUN TO THE BOAT! RUN TO THE BOAT!"

His captain waves a long hook and shouts, "Pull us in, Cooper!"

The cargo is still in the middle of the canal, and oh-so-slowly gliding in toward the dock. Four husky canawlers are poised on the side, ready to jump ashore. Coop runs to the edge of the towpath and strains for the hook. Like a weird, awkward handshake, he and his captain wave their arms, trying to connect.

A small farm wagon pulled by two sweaty horses—foam and spit squirting out their mouths—stops just short of the water, and the two slave catchers—their savage faces eager—jump out and charge toward us.

"Get that nigger kid, too," Big Slaver yells to One Eye. "Don't let her get away!"

I push Beany, then August aside. Pull out my knife, flick it open, and the blade catches a spark of early sunlight. Ready to fight, I jab first at Big Slaver then at One Eye.

"GO, BEANY! RUN, AUGUST!"

Beany grabs August around the waist—she yelps in pain—and they struggle toward the boat, leaving me with the monsters. But those devils don't want me. Big Slaver curves around and lunges at August. One Eye, smelling worse than death, grabs at Beany. Coop stops struggling for the boat hook and races back to help them, but before he gets there One Eye wraps his dirty arm around Beany's neck, shakes her grip off August, and drags her toward the wagon.

August, twisting in the big slave catcher's fists, wails, "NO! NO! I AIN'T GOING BACK!" I jump on Big Slaver and all three of us wrestle up in a pile, kicking, scratching, punching. I see Coop grab One Eye and kick and punch him 'til he lets go of Beany's neck. She falls on the ground, coughing.

My knife flashes again in the morning light. "YAAHHH!" Big Slaver grabs his cheek, cusses, then balls his fist, lunges and punches me square in the face. It makes a sound like August's ax chopping firewood. I fall flat on my back, and my knife bounces away along the dusty towpath.

Blood splatters me from nose to chest, but the pain enrages me. I struggle up and come at Big Slaver again. Diving toward him, I grab his hair, pull his head down, and jerk my knee up into his face. Now *his* nose cracks. He screams, cusses, but instead of coming after me, crawls on hands and knees toward August, who clutches her sides and spits pellets of blood.

Beany crawls toward her mama, too, past Cooper who has One Eye down on the ground, punching him again, again and again. The red eye patch flies off and Coop pounds the empty space.

"Cooper!" The boat captain leans out with the hook, waving like before. Coop leaves One Eye on the ground clutching his head, runs to the water, and this time snags that hook and pulls the boat in to shore.

I scramble in the dirt looking for my knife, gagging and snorting bullets of blood. Big Slaver is on his feet, reaching down to pull August off the ground. He yanks her up by the chain around her wrist, smiling when she screams in pain. Beany grabs her mama's arm, tries to tear her away from the demon and August hangs between them like Ma's Jesus, shrieking, "LET ME GO, BEANY! LET ME GO!"

She wrenches her hand from Beany's and swings a kick between Big Slaver's legs. He blares like a bull and collapses. Then August pushes Beany down so hard she rolls over and over back toward the farm wagon and stomping horses. My hand finds my knife, just as August stumbles past me, heading down the towpath, clutching her sides and hacking up blood. Just as One Eye jumps me from behind.

"MAMA!" Beany claws at the dust.

"NOOOO!" August wails, not turning around. I kick my heavy brogan into One Eye's stomach. He buckles over but comes at me again.

"MAMA, WAIT FOR ME!"

"NOOOO!" A wild, desperate shriek follows August around a turn in the towpath.

"Coop! Mama's running!" Beany scrambles to her feet as the four canawlers jump off the boat. Two yank One Eye off me and start punching him to pulp. The other two grab Big Slaver and hold him while Coop turns his head to mush.

"Mama! Mama! I'm coming."

I lay breathing hard, face in the dirt, but when Beany runs past me I drag myself up and stumble after her around the bend. I see August ahead, on her knees on the ground.

"Mama, boatmen are helping us," Beany calls breathlessly, slowing to a walk.

August's arm swings out in a wide arc, and I see her blue stone knife glitter in the morning sunshine.

"Come back to the boat, Mama! We're leaving."

August's arm swings forward, and I watch the trail of sunshine sparkles cast by the knife blade heading back toward her heart. August jerks with the impact then pitches forward into the dirt.

"AUGUST!" I run to her, stumble, scramble, turn her over, and gather her in my arms. Beany drops to the ground beside us.

"Mama? What did you…? Mama?"

I lay August in the dust. Stare at the blue stone knife sticking out from a patch of purple flowers on her dirty dress. Stare at the blood dribbling out of the hole in her chest, staining the dirty white a muddy red. I wave my hands above her, wanting to pull out the knife. Wanting to yank it out! But…but then the blood will gush.

Beany, weirdly silent beside me, stares.

August is breathing, but the blood oozes faster with each tortured pant. "Oh, Lordy, August, what did you do?" The smell of fresh blood fills my nose and I gag. I feel something building deep inside me and a bellow of rage and fear bursts from my lungs.

"Mama?" I'm startled silent by Beany's voice—so tiny—so different from my own animal howl. My head clears, and I see her finger the blue stone handle gingerly.

"No! Don't touch it! Come on. Let's carry her to the boat."

"Mama's hurt."

"Help me, Beany! Pick her up."

Before I can get my hands under August's shoulders, Beany yanks out the knife.

"NO!" Blood pours out of August's chest like thick cherry syrup. It spreads, soaking her purple-flowered dress, and I see blood flooding the kitchen floor. Ma's blood, kicked out by her drunken husband the night he killed her unborn boy baby. I smell the blood.

"*Cooper!*" I throw my head back and holler, ignoring the pain ricocheting between my ribs. "*Cooper!*" There's a mean creature crawling around inside me, squeezing my heart, tearing my stomach, shocking me sick—scared—mad—terrified.

Beany covers the oozing hole in August's chest with one small hand. August's bloody blade is clamped in her other fist.

I collapse on the ground. Another vicious howl builds inside me. I want to let it out. I want to spit out that mean creature twisting beneath my bones, gnawing at my insides. I want to scream out the sight and smell of blood and the evil, unforgiven crime of revenge.

Footsteps run up behind us.

"Tess, what…? Aw, no!" Coop falls on the ground, lays his hand on August's chest. "Why'd she…? We were winning!" He scoops me into his arms, hushing the low moan rolling up my throat. He touches August again. "I don't think she's breathing." Coop squeezes me tighter, wraps his other strong arm around Beany and pulls her close. We must look like a mound of raw meat to the canawlers who run up and gather around us.

Captain Beale bends over August, feels her neck. "She's breathing, barely. Pick her up, boys. Lay her down in the grass beside the towpath. Come on, Cooper. Get your girls on the boat."

I twist in Coop's grasp. "We can't leave her!"

The captain shakes his head. "Can't take her, hon. She's hurt too badly. Needs a doctor."

I laugh crazily. "Doctor? Stinking doctor won't help her!"

"She won't last an hour on the boat. She might have a chance if she gets medical attention. Put them on the boat, Coop."

"No! We're not leaving August!" When I struggle up, gasping and grimacing from the pain, Beany drapes herself silently, gently across her mama's bloody body.

"We're wasting time, Captain. Both those slave hunters took the boat to Hell," one of the canawlers says. "We gotta get rid of the bodies."

"Put this woman beside the towpath and load those dead men on the boat."

"You're leaving August but taking that scum with us?"

"Tessie, please." Tears puddle in wide cuts on Coop's face. "Help will come."

"Who? When? Your captain says she won't last an hour on his boat. How long will she last in the dirt?"

"She has a chance." The captain says kindly, but I see in his eyes he thinks a very slim one. "Look, folks are coming down the hill. Want to see what the ruckus is about. They'll help her. But we have to get out of here and dump these bodies."

The captain touches Coop's shoulder. "Get the girls on the boat. We'll take care of the woman." The canawlers pull August away from Beany, out of her arms slick with her mama's blood. Beany doesn't peep. I sink into the dirt and roll up in a ball. The long, low moan rolls up through my throat. No. No. We can't leave August.

Cooper picks up Beany. "Come on, Tessie." He nudges me with his boot. "Now!" I stand painfully. My skin, head, arms, legs—everything is cut, bruised, twisted. My eyes bleed. Nose, too. I spit. Spit again. I reach into my mouth, pull something out and throw it on the ground without looking at it. Coop carries Beany to the boat.

"Go on, away from here, Miss," Coop's captain says. "Nothin' to see here." And here's Lucy staring at the men carrying August, her head lolling like a rag doll's, her arms drooping like oars on a rowboat.

"Oh, no." Lucy's voice chokes. "Willow. Tess." Her earthy green eyes flood with tears, but she reaches quickly for Cooper's arm.

"Here." Trembling, Lucy sets a red bag in Beany's wet, limp hand, wraps a cord around her wrist. Presses the girl's bloody fingers around the bag's soft cloth.

"Hold this tight, Willow. Don't let go. It's for you and Tess. Traveling money." She covers her face with her hands and bawls.

"Thanks, Lucy." Coop nods. "We'll pay you back."

"No...no...." She turns away and her shoulders shake like cornstalks in a thunderstorm.

I struggle into the boat, fall onto the deck and hold out my arms. Cooper sinks Beany into my lap, lays her head gently against my shoulder. I wrap myself around her, thinking about the willow branches hiding Beany and August from the world on a Sunday afternoon.

When canawlers dump the slave catchers next to us, a violent shiver rakes my body. I look away and see Coop kneeling beside August on the towpath. He marks Ma's cross over her with a shaky hand. We can't take these dead demons with us and leave August behind. We can't!

"Let's go!" the captain calls. All the canawlers are onboard. Coop unties the rope from a snubbing post and pushes off. I hear a dull slap and a hoot, a slight tug as the mules strain against their harness and the boat moves east.

We slide past August. Is she still barely breathing or has she given up? Past Lucy who takes off her shawl, folds it into a pad and presses it over August's heart. People are pouring down the hill toward the canal. Ma is one of them. Coming from the market? When she reaches the path, she falls to the ground next to Lucy. They exchange a few words then Ma covers August's body with her own shawl. Suddenly the grassy slope is swarming with town folk scurrying to gawk at the towpath attraction. A few lift Ma's shawl to gape at August and she shouts at them. Now Ma's yelling and pointing. Asking someone to get the doctor? Or is it too late? Why did Ma cover August—even her face—with her shawl?

And there's Lucy's pa, laying a heavy arm around his daughter's shoulders, lifting her away from August, pulling her back up the incline to their Dearborn. As we turn the bend, I watch Ma wring her hands and look around frantically, like she's lost something. Or somebody. A thick crowd gathers around August, and I can't see her any longer. Can't see her or Ma.

It wasn't part of our plan for Lucy to return to the towpath with a bulging money sack. She must have had a terrible night. Did she sit up speculating on what her chances of getting to college would be if she dug her ruby velvet bag from its new hiding place and pressed it into Beany's— Willow's—hands? No, Lucy didn't speculate. She knows, like I know, what her chances are. None. And she brought it anyway. Lucy was a mile away but still a part of our battle on the towpath. She's unmarked but bloodied, her college dream dead like August, laid out now on a coffin of wild daisies. Dead. Or soon to be dead.

I settle into the boat's motion and lean my head against a shipping crate. My wounds are vicious. My face a mush of blood and broken bones. Cooper, too, has deep cuts and angry bruises. His forehead is raw from a boot kick, his knuckles split and bleeding. Beany's dark ringlets are twisted and matted with earth, grass and sticks, her face swollen from slaps and sorrow. She doesn't speak. Her dark eyes gaze…where? On that spot in her memory where she last saw her mama? My body is beaten. Beany's soul is brutalized.

I cradle her tenderly and cry for us both. Cooper hovers protectively, tucking a blanket around Beany's shoulders, wiping my bloody face with a rag, while his captain exhorts the hoggee to hurry up those mules.

Our boat plows past Washington Street. I see Lucy jump out of her pa's Dearborn. She's angry. Waves her arms. Shakes her fists. I know she wants to stay with August. Bring the doctor. Force him to save August's life like they'd forced him to fix her shoulder. Her pa turns the Dearborn around and heads back up the street. Miz Manning tries to hold Lucy, but she pulls away and runs into the house. I know where she's going. I know Lucy.

I can't see inside her house, but I know she falls onto her bed and cries hard then softly. She cries until the morning breeze cools her wet, hot face. Then she fills her chest with fresh air, holds it a few seconds then exhales strongly, deliberately.

She rises from her bed, walks to her bureau and takes a cloth bag from the back of the bottom drawer. Sitting down in a straight-backed chair by the window, she pulls out a stack of glove shapes, cut from fabric. Taking out her needle, she threads it carefully, and leaning ever so slightly into the light, begins to stitch. Tiny, patient stitches. One by one. Following in a line. All around the glove.

CHAPTER EIGHTEEN

Cooper stands with his captain in the bow and slaps his neck. "I hate this stretch of canal. Damn gallnippers."

"I don't think you'll be seeing this canal again for a while—Tie those grain sacks to them good and tight, boys—Don't think you should work this end of the canal. Maybe even get off the Erie completely...for a while."

"Captain, you know I love it." Cooper looks anxiously into the older man's face.

"Yeah, I know—Okay, boys, slide them over the side—But you have to think of the girls. Your sister and that little brown one."

"I'll take care of them."

"I'm just saying—Thanks, boys. Those devils won't be going anywhere. Sunk right into the muck, they did. Not that anyone's going to miss those two—I'm just saying, Cooper, that people might be looking for you...after what happened. You really think you killed him?"

Coop touches his raw forehead gingerly. "I'm pretty sure he wasn't breathing when I locked him in the cell."

"Then he's a goner."

"I didn't mean to kill him, just knock him out...for a long enough time." Coop turns from his captain and looks out across the swamp. "I...I don't want to leave the Erie, Captain."

The man puts his hand on Coop's shoulder then drops it when Coop winces in pain. "I know. But look at those girls. Haven't heard a peep out of either of them since we left Seneca Falls—except for the humming from that little one. They just huddle there, clutching each other. Won't eat. Won't drink. They're in bad shape, Cooper. You can't care for them and work the canal."

"They're scared," Coop says softly, glancing over at me and Beany. "Hurt."

"They're broken, son. Take them someplace to heal. Someplace you'll all be safe."

They stand silently. "Rochester?" Coop asks finally.

The captain shakes his head. "Rochester's not far enough. You got big trouble hanging over your head, son. Go someplace far away—YO! Hoggee! Start up those mules, boy! Get us out of this swamp."

"GO, AGGIE! GO, FRANK!" The mules strain into their harnesses, then the captain turns back to stare at me and Beany.

"Lordy, Cooper." He shakes his head. "Get more water and wipe that blood off them. And look, the little one's still holding that dang knife." Cooper wets a rag and wipes at blood that won't stop flowing down my face. "Your sis is swollen so bad she hardly looks human." I know he doesn't mean it unkindly.

Cooper dabs the rag at some dirt on Beany's forehead. She doesn't move. He pushes her curls away from her eyes. She doesn't blink. When he tries to pull the bloody knife from her hand, her fingers tighten.

"What's that she's singing?" the captain asks. "She's been humming nonstop all the way from Seneca Falls."

Coop stands, shakes his head. The captain pulls out a pipe and lights it. "Take them to Canada, son. Take them as far north as you can get."

Water slaps against the cargo as we glide toward the junction of my little skinny canal and the mighty Erie. We're on our way.

But on our way to where? I don't want to go to Canada. Buffalo, that wild boomtown at the Erie's west end, has been my lifelong dream, but now I don't want any part of those ball-bustin' brawls Coop told me about. Not after the battle I fought.

I'm finally getting out of Seneca Falls. I should be happy. But August is dead—or will be soon—and so's...so's Beany. She's breathing here in my arms, but barely. She's cut and marked like me, but damaged in a painfully deeper way. I sense the wound in her. She's dead in her heart, in her soul. I know that tune she's humming. It's the one August sang in her jail cell, one of the kitchen songs Beany and I grew up with. Kitchen songs and warm cherry pies. Fat sausages and bowls of hot mashed potatoes. My bed in the loft. Staring at the stars, planning my escape.

The truth hits me like a sucker punch. I'm finally getting out of Seneca Falls. But how will I survive? Who'll take care of me? Can I take care of Beany?

I tighten my arms around her. Rest my cheek atop her head and stare at Coop's broad back. Will Cooper stick with us? I wriggle uncomfortably. How many times did he promise to visit me and Ma and never showed up. How will we eat if Coop abandons us? And if he ignores his captain's warning, if he plies the Erie, some sheriff will snatch him up once word spreads he's a murderer.

My ribs are a powerful hurt. I know they're busted. My nose, too. How long will it take me to heal? Can I get a job setting type in some western town? Will anybody give me a chance like Miz Bloomer did?

Beany lies like a sack of dried corn in my arms. She's my responsibility now. She's sad and she's sick. Will she ever get well? Can I protect her?

I shiver when the captain calls, "There she is—the mighty Erie Canal."

Yeah, I'm finally getting out of Seneca Falls. But what's next?

Coming in 2010

Wixumlee Is My Salvation

In book two of the Canal Tales Series, Tess and Beany struggle to survive in Buffalo, New York, the Erie Canal's lawless last stop. Beany is kidnapped by a fearsome woman named Wixumlee, who entangles them and Lucy, now living in Oberlin, Ohio, in the bold slave rescues of Harriet Tubman and the Underground Railroad. Tess, turned cowardly by the horrific bloodshed on the towpath, struggles against Wixumlee's questionable influence over Beany and the machinations of her arch enemy Nicky Pappo to win back Beany and regain her own lost courage.

Acknowledgements

I extend deepest thanks to Patricia Petro, my first reader, who offered the first indication that this was a rewarding story, and to subsequent readers Lenore Tracey, who requested a more developed explanation of Tess' emotions at the conclusion, and Erica Mullen, who caught inconsistencies and poor word choices. I'm thankful for the artistic talent of Melissa Bonina, who designed the book's cover and map of western New York, and to Nancy at the historical society in Montour Falls for help with early town names. I'm grateful for the encouragement of friends and strangers, who, after reading excerpts, expressed eagerness to read the entire story, and especially to my kayaking pal Elaine Carter, who promised to buy the first book. I've learned excellent goal-achieving tactics from Go Girl! Dola Burkentine and marketing strategies from The Wilmington Write to Publish Group. Arlene Owens continues to teach me the art of adventure; Lois DeWitt and Cindy Kienitz the value of community action. I thank all the Island Women who have offered me friendship and encouragement. Once again, I acknowledge being blessed with the best husband on earth, my dear George, who throughout the decades has supported my quirks, projects and adventures.

Some of Elizabeth Cady Stanton's quotes and excerpts from newspaper editorials criticizing the First Woman's Rights Convention and its organizers were taken from Elizabeth Griffith's 1984 book *In Her Own Right, the Life of Elizabeth Cady Stanton*. Griffith's book, Stanton's biography *Eighty Years & More* and Miriam Gurko's *The Ladies of Seneca Falls* were excellent sources for assessing the mood and feel of what some called a "petticoat rebellion" and others called "a shocking and unnatural incident." Marvin A. Rapp's *Canal Water and Whiskey* brought the challenges of building the Erie Canal to life and was the source of the canal tune "*Hoggee on the Towpath.*"

CPSIA information can be obtained
at www.ICGtesting.com
Printed in the USA
FFOW04n1403080414
4750FF

Bk 1   PI